ISABELLE DRAKE

For more information contact:
Riverdale Avenue Books
5676 Riverdale Avenue
Riverdale, NY 10471
www.riverdaleavebooks.com

Design by www.formatting4U.com
Cover by Scott Carpenter

Digital ISBN: 9781626014763
Print ISBN: 9781626014756

Previously published by Cerridwen Press, September, 2009
Second edition, August 2018

Praise for Cowboy for Hire

Winner of the 2009 Psyche Award Winner

"Okay, I love cowboys and Arizona, so *Cowboy for Hire* really captured my heart. I love the dialogue and the way the chemistry works between Victoria and Lang. Their relationship springs to life and leaps into the reader's heart. Isabelle Drake is a great storyteller."

—Cherokee, *Coffee Time Romance*

"… overall, this was a fun book to read full of dreams and real life.

—Terri, *Night Owl Romance*

"I found *Cowboy for Hire* by Isabelle Drake to be a fun story. I was instantly drawn to Lang. He is the type of cowboy hero every gal dreams of. Victoria keeps him on his toes and he stays in a state of constant confusion. I thoroughly enjoyed reading *Cowboy for Hire* and look forward to reading more books by Ms. Drake."

—Manic Readers

"*Cowboy for Hire* by Isabelle Drake is a funny, fast read. When I picked up this book I wasn't sure what to expect. I have always loved a good cowboy story and was not disappointed. I would recommend this cowboy romance to any reader and will be looking for more books by Ms. Drake."

—Kim N, *Romance Junkies*

"Ms. Drake has a wonderful way of writing. I loved *Cowboy for Hire*. I found that it flowed amazingly well, and I had no problem whatsoever in following along. Victoria and Lang seem to be opposites, but in fact are …well, I'll let you read the book and see for yourselves."

—Alyna Couture, *The Romance Studio*

Praise for Isabelle Drake

SATISFACTION GUARANTEED

"I highly recommend this book to all who like to experience real-life people with a strong attraction which has some great ups and downs. It is a good book which I think you will certainly enjoy and remember for some time to come."

—Brenda Talley, *The Romance Studio*

"This is the first book I have read by Isabelle Drake and was really surprised how well she handles the relationship between Elizabeth and Jack. Their dates were very sweet and very fun. Plus, when Jack and Elizabeth finally get under the sheets, their lovemaking is explosive and intimate. For a guaranteed sexy romance, *Satisfaction Guaranteed* is one I would recommend you pick up."

—Katie, *Romance Junkies*

EVERGLADES W ILDFIRE

"EVERGLADES WILDFIRE is a BUZZWORTHY BOOK!"

"Isabelle Drake's novel, EVERGLADES WILDFIRE is a scorcher!"

—Shon Bacon, SisterDivas Magazine

4 Cups—a keeper—from Coffee Time Romance
"Isabelle Drake writes a vivid tale of hot sex and the inner struggles of the characters as they fight their love for each other. Amber's conflicting need for a safe secure family and her attraction to the handsome rancher are intense. Rick's attempts to over come his past while he fights to keep the woman he loves will keep the reader glued to the page. The sex scenes are very hot. The plot twists keep the reader guessing. I enjoyed this book and I look forward to reading more by this author."

—Candy, *Coffee Time Romance*

"Hot, sexy and comfortable all rolled into one. The bad-boy with a gold heart meets the one girl that can make it all come out right has been retold in a luscious setting that left me sweating for all the right reasons with enough new elements to have me hanging on every word. Ms. Drake provides a smorgasbord of emotions for the reader to feast upon and leave replete."

—Keely Skillman, *EcataRomance Reviews*

4 Unicorns—Enchanted in Romance
"The sexual tension that simmers below the surface of *Everglades Wildfire* is amazing. Ms. Drake does a great job of showing their past without getting bogged down in the details. The characters are very sympathetic and it's easy to identify with Amber's struggle between the two men in her life. It's a fun read."

—Natalie, *Enchanted in Romance*

"Isabelle Drake creates a sensual, steamy backdrop for her *Everglades Wildfire*. This is a complex and intriguing story... The sex scenes will get you so hot and bothered that you'll want to make sure you've got the air conditioning turned up! The lush scenery and surprisingly complex story will grab your attention and keep you hooked. Read Ms. Drake's *Everglades Wildfire*, you'll enjoy it."

—Trang, *Fallen Angels Reviews*

FATE UNBOUND

Night Owl Reviews TOP PICK

"Isabelle Drake's latest release, Fate Unbound is an extremely erotic look into some of lives of Greek gods and goddesses.

"Ms. Drake has penned a fascinating story that will captivate readers right from the very first page. Her characters are believable, intelligent and captivating. The storyline is unique, intriguing and enchanting. The sexual tension between the main characters is so rcd hot that sparks seem to fly right off the page. I am delighted to add this book to my keeper collection and recommend this book to others."

—Heather, *Night Owl Reviews*

"Full of intriguing characters and an oracle's declaration, Ms. Drake delves into Taryn and Adrian's story with abandon and delivers a sensual twist that will leave you breathless."

—Dawn, *Love Romances & More*

Dear Reader,

This reissue of *Cowboy for Hire* is unchanged, so this romance story is still as sweet as it was when released a few years ago. I'm thrilled about that. For me, it's like coming home. Some of my readers may not know this about me, but I wrote sweet, traditional romances before creating my first erotic romance, *Everglades Wildfire*. I was even a Romance Writers of America Golden Heart finalist in the Traditional Romance category.

It's natural for people to ask writers of erotic romance why they write such sexually explicit stories. Interestingly, people don't ask that of sweet romance authors. I think that's because it's apparent—everyone loves a love story. That's what *Cowboy for Hire* is—a tender, light-hearted, sometimes funny, sometimes poignant, story about two people getting past the tangles of their past and getting tangled together.

Thank you for coming along for another ride with me. I'm all over social media and easy to find. Come join me there.

Isabelle
August, 2018

Chapter One

Lang Thompson eased his foot off the worthless brake pedal and waited for the red Arizona dust to clear. A board swung above the cab of his truck, once, twice, three times. The rusty nail holding it gave up the fight and the weathered two-by-four smacked across the hood with a weary thump.

One more dent wasn't going to matter.

He pushed back his beat-up Stetson, mumbling a string of words that in his childhood would've earned him an afternoon in the milk house. He didn't need this.

Outside his window a hairy, black Australian shepherd barked and waved its tail.

"You don't need to tell me, I see the mess."

For a split second he considered backing out and leaving. The way the place looked, the owner probably wouldn't even notice the new gaping hole.

No, he didn't want any unfinished business hanging over his head when he hit the highway again to head south, away from the miserable memories he'd left behind. There was that and the fact that his conscience had an unfortunate way of popping up at the worst times.

He glanced down at the animal now sitting among the rubble that used to be the side of a barn. A tired, seen-better-days barn, but a barn nonetheless.

For the sake of his furry witness, he held back another string of words unfit for delicate ears as he shoved the door open and stepped out. He leaned against the truck and yanked his hat down to block out the afternoon sun. The owner had to be around somewhere.

"I guess I should've hung a no parking sign there."

Lang turned to the shapely outline in the shadows. His bad luck kept getting worse. A woman. He didn't want to shoot the breeze with a bored rancher's wife.

"If you'll tell me where to find your husband, I'll straighten this out with him."

As she moved into the sunshine Lang tried to convince himself he didn't see her thick blonde hair or deep, blue eyes. He didn't notice the way her breasts strained against that plain white T-shirt tucked neatly into her faded jeans, either. And that bolt of physical awareness that shot straight to his cock? It didn't exist.

A blindingly bright smile spilt across her sun-kissed face. "I can't do that."

No, those sweet lips didn't really have an effect on him either. But just to be sure, he stepped away as she came closer. "Do what?"

Raising her hand to shield her eyes from the desert sun, she glanced over her shoulder toward the mess. "Did you plow into my barn because you suffer from memory loss?"

Lang turned toward his truck. He had indeed plowed into the barn. *Her barn.* "Your barn?"

She nodded, then reached down to rub the dog's ears, giving him the perfect opportunity to look down her shirt. Was that a white bra with pink lace trim?

Damn he loved lace.

Forcing his gaze back to her face, he asked, "You don't have a husband I can talk things over with?"

Sunlight blinked off the golden strands of her hair as she shook her head and scratched under the animal's chin. Her silence didn't make sense. Why wasn't she pissed? "Look, ma'am, I'm really sorry—"

While waving her hands to cut him off, she moved closer, her sexy, long legs making short work of the distance. "You don't need to explain right now."

Judging from the tilt of her head and the welcome in her eyes, he was missing some piece of a puzzle.

But what?

He stamped out his curiosity. He only wanted to take care of business, then get back on the road and find that ranch for sale his cousin Cole had badgered him into looking over. With that out of the way, he'd get back to his real goal, which was putting as much distance between the remnants of his old life and himself as possible. He tugged his gaze away from her all-too-easy-on-the-eyes face, glanced around but soon found himself looking her way again. "Where am I anyway?"

Her delicate eyebrows knotted together and her shoulders dropped. "You didn't come about the ad for work?"

"Work?" He shook his head. "No. I was trying to turn around, get back on the freeway."

Her kissable pink lips curved weakly, the glimmer in her eyes faded but didn't go out completely. "You're at The Circle Cat Ranch."

"And where is that?"

"Cactus Junction." She dipped her head the other way and a few tempting strands of silken hair slipped over her shoulder. "You do know what state you're in?"

3

Arizona. Only a couple of hours from the Mexican border.

Her gaze circled his face, considering, then dropped lower, assessing. He straightened, planting his legs wide enough to place the bulge in his pants front and center. If she insisted on getting a good look at him, he might as well give her a view worth the effort.

As though she realized she was rudely looking him over like he was a colt on the auction block, she brought her attention back to his face and tried to cover her actions with a smile as she spoke. "You look like you could use a drink. I know I could." She brushed past him without waiting for a reply. "Come on up to the house and have some lemonade."

That place his cousin was so hot for them to buy was in Cactus Junction. At least he didn't have much farther to go.

Not that he *wanted* to buy a place and start all over but Cole had cajoled him until he'd agreed to at least look it over. A promise is a promise. Even to a cousin like Cole.

The woman's hips swayed invitingly as she strode toward the house. Each determined stride called to some better left unspoken part of him.

He grumbled and tore his gaze away. He'd written complicated entanglements with women off. For good.

The screen door smacked shut after she disappeared inside.

Why did it seem like the last shred of control he had over his life was slipping away? The hot wave of lust pooling in his gut shouted a warning, telling him to forget his so-called integrity and take the chance

4

that once he got on the road he wouldn't need brakes any time soon. He could always coast to a stop.

He groaned. All those hours in the milk house taught him more than to mind his tongue. He had to stick around and settle the issue at hand. That ranch for sale wasn't going anywhere. With a quick glance down to be sure he wasn't wearing any of his fast food breakfast on his shirt, Lang headed after the woman and the dog.

* * *

Victoria Marana dug through the half empty boxes covering her kitchen floor. The moving company had delivered them days ago. She hadn't unpacked because she'd been too busy hauling wood and pounding nails. Having things like pitchers handy hadn't even crossed her mind.

She twisted to peek out the window. With each slow swing of his long, lean legs, the cowboy ambled closer to the house. Worry nagged her and she frowned.

The want ad for a ranch hand had been in the paper for two weeks and not one person had stopped by. When she'd spotted the man looking around, she'd been sure he was there about the job. Admittedly, his actions so far didn't recommend him, but he looked strong and capable and she didn't have time to be picky.

She turned back to her search, pushing kitchen utensils out of the way until she found a plain glass pitcher. As she shoved aside some half-full grocery bags, she admired the newly installed stainless steel counter tops. They gleamed in the sunlight with promise for the future.

Success dangled in front of her, giving her just enough encouragement to hold tight to the hope that The Circle Cat would be ready to open on schedule. Though she'd been working hard for weeks, the list of necessary repairs never seemed to shrink. She and Hank, the old man who came with the place, could only do so much.

Heavy footfalls on her porch, followed by what she'd come to recognize as the squeaky hinges of the swing, made her heart pick up speed.

If only the cowboy had come about the ad. One more person would make such a difference. As she picked through the groceries looking for the lemonade mix, she realized her father was right. Running a business was a lot harder than she'd expected.

Her determination could only get her so far. She needed another pair of hands to get her the rest of the way. After carefully measuring the mix, then adding the water, she grabbed a long wooden spoon and stirred.

She could charm the cowboy into staying. He definitely had the look of a single man. Bachelors loved attention, right?

Sex appeal always worked for her sister. Why wouldn't it work for her? So what if she'd never tried to charm a man into doing anything. That was no reason to reject the idea. She was desperate and an able-bodied man sat on her porch.

Before she could talk herself out of the notion, she pulled in a deep breath, put on a smile, grabbed the glasses with one hand and the pitcher with the other. There was just enough space between the kitchen and the door to practice a sexy, you-know-you-want-it walk. The exaggerated sway made droplets of lemonade splash onto the planked floor.

She pushed the screen door open with her hip, then arched against the doorjamb to offer him a clear view of the outline of her breasts. She'd read enough of her stepmother's copies of *Cosmopolitan* to know he was supposed to be ogling her just then. But he wasn't.

Instead, he was staring at the freshly whitewashed porch railing. Apparently he didn't read *Cosmo*. Clearing her throat to get his attention didn't seem very alluring.

Obviously, he wasn't going to cooperate easily. She let the door slam behind her as she stepped over to the table and set the glasses down. She filled them, then dropped into the chair across from him.

Promise chose that moment to reappear. The dog climbed up the steps, padded across the porch and settled by the cowboy. Eyeing the dog, the man muttered thanks as he picked up one of the glasses and then took a long drink. Victoria watched the greedy way he swallowed, wondering vaguely why she couldn't take her eyes off him. The muscular arch of his throat, his suntanned fingers curved so strongly around the delicate glass.

Her gaze fell to the collar of his shirt, then lower to the tiny buttons holding it closed. She could pop those open easily enough and run her fingers across the hard planes of his chest and circle around to his back.

Hold on, girl.

She pulled her thoughts together and back to the problem at hand. Convincing him to stick around and work. She'd better act fast. He didn't look like the kind of man who waited long for anything.

Hoping to snag his attention, she shoved her shoulders back and ran her tongue across her lips. But now he was staring at the glass.

"About the barn… " He rambled on about the brakes in his truck and how he hadn't been getting much sleep lately.

Victoria tried to listen but she had a hard time understanding his explanation about fluid and lines while her own problem pressed in. Valuable time was slipping away. If only he'd stop going on about his stupid truck and look at her.

Catch his eye!

Shoving her ribcage forward, she crossed her legs in a slow, seductive way but nearly lost her balance in the process. Instead of being properly—silently—embarrassed, a nervous chuckle slipped out.

"You think that's funny?"

"No, um, yes?" What had he been saying? The empty cloud in her brain didn't hold that bit of information. All she could think about was the solid line of his jaw covered by the stubble of a two-day beard. Instead of making him look scruffy, it made him rugged and appealing. Set off his dark eyes, even drew attention to the unruly locks of hair curling around his muscular neck.

With his solid arms set across his sturdy chest, he looked as powerful as the workers on her father's carpentry crews, except this man had raw sex appeal packed into every square inch.

He wasn't a collection of good parts—he was the whole package. How had she failed to notice that he was a walking ad for sex? The only explanation was that she'd been distracted by her plans for The Circle Cat. A worthwhile cause but still…

This guy could take on wild forces of nature and come up the winner every time. Her gaze slid down the length of his powerful thighs to his worn Ropers, curved up, lingered on the solid bulge under his zipper, paused to take in his taut, flat stomach and then inched its way back up.

Curiosity tugged at her heart and anticipation quickened her blood. Her eyes met his and for a split second she was sure he was thinking something— about her. Caught up in her own revelations about him, she didn't look away. Couldn't look away. Long seconds ticked past, awareness sizzled in the warm desert air.

Sure, she'd written marriage off, but spending time with a man like him, on her own terms, well… that had plenty of appeal. She *had* promised herself some fun and this guy had fun written all over him, in big, Las Vegas style, neon letters. The muscles in his jaw flexed, hard and determined. Maybe not *fun*, exactly, a good time—yes, definitely that.

He shoved his hat back and the tiny trace of a smile lifted his capable, kissable mouth. The gaze of his liquid brown eyes met hers, causing a jolt of electricity to skim across her nerves, swirl down her stomach and settle between her legs.

"Which is it, yes or no?"

His question. Right.

Did she think what was funny?

To keep his thoughts going in the right direction and cover up the fact that she wasn't listening to the business about his brakes, she tilted her head and lifted her eyebrows. "How about maybe?"

She widened her smile. His dropped.

What was she doing wrong?

"Listen. All I want to do is straighten out this barn problem, Miss—"

"Marana." She lowered her voice, "But you can just call me Victoria."

His eyes narrowed and his shoulders tensed. He leaned back, efficiently rolling the glass in his competent hands. The harder she tried to win him over the more he pulled back. If she weren't so frustrated, she would've laughed.

Never one to give up once she got settled on an idea, she ignored his lack of cooperation and kept leaning toward him invitingly.

He shifted sideways. "As in Marana Construction from Phoenix?"

"That's my father's company," she replied, putting emphasis on *father*. That easy life she'd eagerly left behind was a thing of the past. She'd come to The Circle Cat to be her own woman, to make her own dreams come true and have some unrestricted fun in the process.

She was done letting herself be defined by her father's reputation and controlling personality and ready to uncover what she'd been missing out on with members of the opposite sex. Simply put, she was tired of experiencing fun, spur-of-the-moment flings and hot, fast-paced affairs through friends.

All she needed was the right man... and fate may have just delivered him.

Chapter Two

Lang held in a groan as he set the glass on the table and stood. Dealing with Victoria Marana was worse than dealing with a stir-crazy rancher's wife. At least a rancher's wife would understand about broken dreams and an empty wallet. There was no way he could explain to a pampered rich girl that he had no money to pay for the damage he'd done. She'd laugh in his face.

He knew that much, and a lot more, when it came to women who were used to getting whatever they wanted, whenever they wanted it. All that high maintenance didn't come cheap. And it wasn't easy to deliver.

Whoa.

Something didn't make sense.

He put the empty glass on the table and slipped his hands into his back pockets. What was a pretty thing like her doing on a broken down ranch anyway? "What're you doing out here?"

"This is my place," she replied wistfully, gazing around at the vast expanse of space.

"I figured that." He braced his hands on the railing, leaned back. "What are you doing here?"

Her vibrant eyes glittered as she set down her drink. "I bought it a couple of weeks ago. I'm fixing it up."

"You just bought it?"

"That's right. From the Perez's."

Lang swallowed against the bewildering pang of regret swelling his throat as the truth of things made itself known. No doubt this ranch was the very one Cole had told him to look over. "You bought it from a man named Pete Perez?" he asked, even though he already knew the answer.

"That's right. You know him?"

Her cheerful enthusiasm grated on his nerves. "No. Heard of him though." He couldn't tell if the emotion squeezing his chest was misplaced disappointment at losing out on the ranch or resentment that this spoiled, citified girl was the new owner.

Lang tried to look on the bright side, that with the place off the market and he wouldn't have to spend time explaining to Cole why he didn't want to start all over again, but for some reason the bright side was surprisingly dark.

She brushed her sleek hair back with a precise wave of her slender fingers. "I open for business next week."

He recognized that flash of excitement in her eyes. It was something he knew all about. She had the look of someone who had a vision and believed she could make it come true.

When he remained silent, she added, "The Circle Cat's going to be the best dude ranch in Arizona."

He spun on his heels to take a more thorough look. For the first time he noticed the recent repairs dotting the place. Several of the barn windows were new and the fence along the drive showed signs of mending.

The buildings out back could be bunkhouses, the barn he'd run into could hold plenty of horses. Once it was repaired. The old house probably had a dining room big enough to seat a dozen or so hungry tourists.

Lang rubbed his bristled jaw. The yard sure was nice enough. Tall Ponderosa pines and aspens framed the whole place pretty well. He could see the potential.

If he was a dreamer. Which he definitely was not.

Not anymore, anyway.

He roped in his rambling thoughts and brought them back to the problem of the barn. Thanks to the disaster his life had become he couldn't pay for repairs. He couldn't leave the mess either. On one hand Victoria Marana didn't need his money, on the other he didn't want to be indebted to a wealthy man's daughter.

Still…

Although he couldn't imagine how, trouble would crop up somewhere down the road. That was the problem. Victoria Marana's kind of woman knew how to zero in on a man's weakness and then, using a surprise attack, work it to her advantage.

His cheating ex-wife, Lori Anne, had done that very thing and he wasn't going to let that hard-learned lesson go to waste. No sir, the anguish of losing his ranch, everything else he owned—including his prized horses—well, that wasn't something he could live through twice.

Think with your brain man, not your cock.

That was his new mantra and he'd better remember it.

Gorgeous Lori Anne had battered his heart and torn apart his pride, but deep down he was still the same man. That meant buried under all his pain, he still had integrity.

That integrity left him with only one choice. A choice that was going to keep him from the Mexican border a little while longer. "I'll fix the barn." The dog stretched out of the way as Lang leaned around the corner to study the damage. "It'll only take a couple of days."

She didn't say anything.

Did she expect him to pull out a checkbook and take care of it that way?

He turned to find her dazzling eyes assessing him from under long, feathery lashes. Her gaze flickered across his shoulders, then back to his face. That needy feeling in his gut came back and he started wondering if she heated up as quickly. Or would she make him take things slow and steady, stroking her until they both ached for release?

Maybe sticking around wasn't such a good plan after all. His wandering gaze skimmed over her cotton covered curves, lingering on the points of her nipples, then skimming down to the zipper on her jeans.

No maybe about it. Being around that sweetly sexy woman was the worst idea he'd had in months and he had enough horse sense to know he'd be regretting his decision soon enough.

For now, he had no choice. He'd be staying.

Victoria moved to stand beside him. "At least you didn't hit a supporting beam."

He stepped away from the railing—and the delicate citrus scent he was beginning to recognize as hers. "Is it a deal, Miss Marana? I'll take care of the damage myself?"

She leaned back on the rail like a sleepy kitten and grinned. "You never did tell me your name."

If he didn't know better, he'd think she was flirting with him. Couldn't be though, because a woman with her background would be a whole lot more skillful at snaring a man's interest. But the odd combinations Victoria kept offering up, well, they were just that. Odd. Hot—cool—genuine—forced… in short, a little weird. Cute and damned sexy—if he was interested—which he was not. Not quite the well-practiced, come-hither package he'd expect from someone like her.

Twisting from side-to-side, she asked his name again.

Keeping a watchful eye on her, he answered, "Lang Thompson, from north of Phoenix." He folded his arms across his chest, a lame attempt to protect himself from the stir-crazy affect she had on him and stared hard at her.

Again, her gaze zigzagged over him, blazing a hot trail of want and leaving a path of over-sensitive nerve endings. "It isn't necessary for you to do the work."

Now what did she mean by that? He wasn't good enough to do the work? Indecision sparked through him, stamped it out, grumbling. "I caused the damage. I'll make it right."

She blinked and then turned her attention to the mess across the yard.

So now he gets the cold shoulder? "You have a problem with me doing the work?" he asked, not willing to allow her the upper hand.

"No, it'll be a straightforward job," she answered so softly she could've been talking to herself. But then she spun and stretched out her arm. "We have a deal, Lang Thompson."

Lang accepted her hand but because his body wasn't listening to the don't-look, don't-touch messages his brain kept sending out, he hurried through the motion, then pulled back. The road of sizzling, physical attraction was rough and filled with holes and he didn't want any part of it.

There was still one more thing. "You won't mind me sleeping in my truck? I'll move it behind the barn so nobody will see it from the road."

Her eyebrows pulled together. "Why would you want to sleep there?"

"Like I said, I'm not from around here."

Her soft mouth rounded into an "o" and her eyes brightened. "You willing to work extra for meals?"

Home-cooked food instead of gas station burritos?

He nodded.

"You'll stay here but you're not going to sleep in your truck." The flirtatious smile reappeared. "I want you comfortable and well rested so you can earn that food," she added with exaggerated sweetness.

He clenched his jaw, fighting against the picture starting to form in his mind. Silky strands of long blonde hair, sliding across a naked woman's shoulders… a woman's hand reaching for him as she climbed across his lap and mounted up, sliding his cock into her tight pussy, then throwing her hair back as she rode him…

Lang shook his leg to chase away the stirrings of an erection. There was no way she was about to suggest what he was imagining.

16

Or was there?

"You'll sleep with Hank, my hired hand."

Lang nearly choked. The hazy image in his head turned into a nightmare. Instead of a sexy blonde in his arms, tangled among the sheets, he held a weathered cowhand.

To add to his disgust, Victoria laughed.

The light, feminine sound skittered across his nerves, making his heart pound harder.

After a hearty chuckle at his expense, she said, "Don't look like that. There's more than one bed." She stepped off the porch, beckoning him with a wave. "Come on, I'll show you."

He glared and stayed put.

"I have a bunkhouse ready. Doesn't a nice, cozy bed sound better than the cab of your truck?"

Lang was having a hard time shaking off the original sleeping arrangement his traitorous imagination had cooked up. There was no telling what images might appear if he got close to her again, so he stayed put, unwilling to leave the safe distance he maintained on the porch.

She rooted her boots in the dirt and squared her shoulders. "I can be as hardheaded as you, cowboy."

There was no point in arguing. Obviously the woman had a stubborn streak. Besides, he'd already spent too many nights cramped in his truck. The idea of just one night in a real bed, even if it was alone, had a lot of appeal.

He eyed the sleeping dog enviously. "I'm coming."

Apparently satisfied that she was getting what she wanted, she headed back the way they'd come. Lang

17

hung behind a bit, then thought better of it when he found himself admiring the way her jeans molded to the perfect shape of her ass. Strong, firm, hips meant to be held. His hands were just the right size.

Because of the enticing scent spinning around her, walking beside her wasn't much easier on his overly charged state. Having the hots for Miss Marana would only cause trouble and he'd had enough of that to last him a lifetime.

Once they got to the barn mess, he slipped into his truck, carefully pulled it out of the rubble, then rolled it around back. Before he climbed out, he grabbed his duffle bag.

Out of the corner of his eye, he caught Victoria watching his every move. The hesitant, shy way she studied him quickened his blood even more than the showy smiles she'd offered earlier.

He doubted she realized her wide eyes and slightly parted lips revealed keen interest. Unable to keep himself from pointing out her obvious behavior, he paused, letting her know he had all day to stand there while she drank her fill.

She blinked and jerked away but not before he saw an honest, pink glow brighten her cheeks, giving her complexion a just-kissed look and putting his senses on full alert. Lang muttered a curse. What was he doing? He was supposed to be tending that fence around his heart, not hacking away at it with a newly sharpened ax.

They approached the buildings he'd seen from the barn. Up close they didn't look nearly as rough. Some boards had been replaced and newly laid, stone paths connected a long walk that ran the length of them. All they needed now was a good, thick coat of paint.

When she paused beside the large bunkhouse, he realized she'd been watching him check out the buildings. The pride in her delicate, surprisingly strong, shoulders was unmistakable.

"I'm going to paint each one a different color and decorate them with different themes." She stretched her tanned arm, pointing. "The first is The Wranglers Restplace, next is Gunfighters Lodge, then Cactus Cabin."

"What about that one?" Lang indicated one she'd left out, a small house nestled among some pines.

There was the shortest pause before she answered with a soft voice, "That's Paradise Hideaway."

The tiny place was probably only big enough for a bed. That relentless picture of himself twisted in the sheets with a sexually charged woman popped back into his head. He glared at the tempting blonde causing the image. She wasn't looking at him at all.

A day dreamy expression had gentled her face. A warning bell pealed into Lang's muddled head. His male instincts knew what was coming even before the words slipped across her lips.

"It's for the honeymooners," she said with a wistful sigh.

He pulled hard on his thoughts. She was talking about a different kind of paradise altogether. The make-believe kind that women made up so they could talk men into doing things they didn't want any part of.

Commitment and marriage.

Well, he tried 'em both but they weren't for him.

It was way past time for him to take control of the conversation. "You were going to show me the bunkhouse?"

When she turned back to him, a trace of the longing remained. For a spilt second he wished she'd

19

look at him with that vulnerable expression again. Then his sanity returned. All he wanted was to fix his mess and get across that border. He'd call his cousin from Mexico, tell him the place was already sold, then find himself a dark cantina with an endless supply of cheap, mind-numbing drinks. Now, thanks to Victoria, he was going to need a generous supply of willing women too.

She opened the door of the bunkhouse, then stepped in and held it for him. He moved over the threshold, careful not to let their fingers brush when he took the door from her.

There were four sets of sturdy wooden bunk beds, twice as many dressers and a long table with eight chairs in the back. A fat, wood-burning stove, guaranteed to keep the place warm enough in cold weather, squatted in the center of the room. After the nights he'd spent in the truck, it looked like a slice of heaven.

She smoothed the white and red checked cloth covering the table. "There's plenty of room for you."

"Hank is your only hand?"

"For now." She shrugged. "He came with the ranch."

An awkward silence stretched between them. The room was too quiet, the walls too tight. Out in the open it was much easier to deal with his body's reaction to the hankerings he was desperately trying to squelch.

He struggled for something to say. Anything that would get his attention away from the round swells of her breasts and the gentle curve of her trim waistline. Anything that would get him to stop thinking about acting on the coming-out-of-nowhere, all-too-impulsive, surge of hormones making his blood pulse in all the wrong places. "It's good to have somebody who knows the place," he muttered to fill in the silence.

Biting her sweet, full, bottom lip, she nodded and looked away. "He's been great."

Lang shifted, his boots crunching on the pebbles scattered by the door. Victoria's face clouded with uncertainty while she fidgeted with the edge of the tablecloth.

She stepped back, pointing past the bunk beds. "If you want to get cleaned up, there's a shower behind that door."

Curiosity nudged him. Earlier she'd been teasing him, coming on strong, yet he was certain that when it came to men she was still a filly—all full of charm and energy but at the first attempt at being handled, she'd sidestep with the speed of a road runner.

He watched her from the corner of his eye, the same way she eyed him. Sly and appraising.

A bit of the devil got the better of him and for the first time in weeks, a real grin tugged at his mouth. With a quick jerk, he yanked his shirttail out and slipped apart the top two buttons.

Her quick intake of air confirmed his theory. Her blue eyes widened, "Wha-what— What're you... doing?"

"I'm getting undressed." Sure, she'd be dashing out the door quick enough but it felt good to put some of his energy to use. He loosened two more buttons, grinned wickedly, loosened two more.

Her wobbly gaze fell to his nearly bare chest. "Why?"

After he freed the last of the buttons, he whipped the shirt off, tossed it onto his bag. "I'm taking you up on your offer."

While she watched, as still as a possum playing

dead, he unbuckled his belt. He popped open the top button of his jeans.

She backed up, her gaze darting down to the white band of his briefs.

He winked and smiled the easy way he did at the dance hall to draw out even the shyest girl. "Your offer to get cleaned up."

A flush of red stained her cheeks. "Of course. Well," she scurried for the door. "Yes, um, I'll see you later. When you're… dressed… "

With that, she dashed through the doorway, closing the heavy wood door tightly behind her.

For the first time in weeks, he laughed.

As much as she'd tried, and she certainly had, that woman was no temptress. His hostess was a fraud. A sweet, sexy-as-sin-on-Saturday-night, fraud.

He kicked the last of his clothing toward a bunk and strutted to the shower. The warm desert air from an open window whispered across his bare skin, reminding him too much of a woman's touch. It caressed a man everywhere at once. Without even trying.

The hot water wouldn't be necessary until tomorrow morning. Maybe not even that soon, if his night dreams picked up where the day dreams had started.

At least he wouldn't have to worry about her flirtatious game. He laughed as the icy water ran down his back. His virtue was safe during his stay at The Circle Cat.

Chapter Three

Victoria marched away from the bunkhouse with the sound of rich, male laughter flooding her ears. Those hard wooden beds and that solid planked floor never looked intimate when she stopped by to talk with Hank. That old man always made the place feel like a stage set from that old TV show, *Gunsmoke*.

With Lang Thompson standing there, filling the place up with his bare chest, it looked more like a photo backdrop from one her sister's tattered *Playgirl* magazines. She ought to know, she'd looked those over a few more times than she'd care to admit.

She raised her palms to her cheeks where the heat of embarrassment still lingered. What an idiot he must think her to be, the way she gaped at his chest, nearly swooning at the sight of those magnificent masculine curves. Staring at the tight, smooth skin of his abs and wondering how it would feel pressed against her. If she weren't so mortified, she'd be laughing at her awkward reaction too.

After rounding the corner of the house, she climbed the front porch steps to snatch their glasses and half-empty pitcher. She grumbled as she stalked through the house. He thought he was so funny. Stupid, infuriating man.

She didn't have a choice about agreeing that he do the repairs. The Circle Cat couldn't open for business with a smashed up barn. And she'd even gotten something out of the deal—he'd agreed to work for food. How many times had she heard her father say the trick to business success was taking opportunities where you find them? See, she reasoned, she was simply being an effective businesswoman.

Getting the ranch fixed up mattered a lot more than some rambling cowboy's opinion of her.

The glasses clinked when she set them in the sink and the lemonade sloshed when she slid it into the refrigerator. What about her pride? Didn't that count?

What about that undeniable mutual attraction?

True, she didn't have oodles of practiced skills, well… none actually being the one who made the first move. But she knew instant chemistry when it flashed in her face. He'd felt that sizzle in the air too, she was sure of it.

So why had he taken it upon himself to… What exactly *had* he been trying to accomplish with that strip tease?

Prove that she wasn't as experienced as he was?

Excuse me if I have standards and don't whip my clothes off every time a magnificent male specimen undresses in front of me.

Standards or no standards, the pitiful truth was, Victoria had never whipped her clothes off for any guy. Gorgeous or otherwise.

That was something she planned on correcting, sooner rather than later.

She stomped outside to the side porch and dropped onto the top step. Sure, she had a full afternoon of work ahead but those chores could wait a short while. Sometimes a girl needed a minute to sort things out.

Promise trotted up, settled and blinked her dark eyes.

"What do you think? Is he still laughing?" She rubbed the animal's thick fur.

It wasn't as though she didn't have experience with men. In the past year or so, she'd gone on dozens of dates. Sure, they'd all been upstanding, prosperous business types her father and stepmother handpicked for her but they still counted as men.

Bossy, know-it-all men. Men who thought they knew who she was without even taking the time to find out.

Was there any other kind?

Each of those evenings had ended with the inevitable chat with her seated on the overstuffed chair in her father's den, while he and her stepmother debated the man's eligibility. It had taken her way too long to figure out that her parents thought it was high time for her to settle down.

They'd done the same thing with her sister, Katherine, so she really should've seen it coming. One thing was certain, Victoria did not want to end up like her older sibling, married—with her whole future already mapped out.

Unlike her sister, her life would be about choices, not limitations. She'd hopped into the driver's seat and intended to stay there. Mistakes, they'd be her own. Things done right, she'd get the credit.

That restlessness that had sent her packing, searching for something bigger… she wasn't about to ignore it. Life was too short for regrets of what might've been and the world was too big for her not to at least try to carve out her own slice.

Settling down with a man was the last thing on her mind. Her plans included hard work, achieving her goal and enjoying herself—however she saw fit— while she was at it. Getting The Circle Cat back on its feet and filled with satisfied guests would be her adventure. Something she'd do on her own terms, something to be proud of. Something to show everyone back home that she was more than just a rich man's daughter.

Her personal life?

She wasn't about to ignore that. No matter what Lang thought, there would be some hot times in her future. Her *immediate* future. And if he wasn't willing, then she'd find someone else.

Marriage? She'd canceled out that possibly when she wrote the check for the down payment on her dream. But carefree experiences with men of her own choosing—yes.

"It seems we have a new doorway in the barn. You didn't like the other one, Miss Marana?"

Victoria doused her daydreaming and waved at Hank as he rambled up the walk. "Afternoon, Mr. Cartwright."

He slipped off his hat, frowning. "I told you to call me Hank."

"I will," she grinned up at him, "But I wish you'd call me Victoria."

He attempted a disapproving scowl but one side of his mouth fought a grin. She might never get the old man to call her by her first name, that didn't mean she'd give up trying.

She gestured to the barn. "A cowboy had some trouble with his truck brakes."

Hank's bushy eyebrows shot up. "He stop by looking for work?"

"No but that's what he's found. He's offered to take care of the repairs himself and agreed to work more for board."

Hank twisted his cheek. "Does that suit you, having him around?"

The image of Lang, bare-chested and unbuttoning his pants, burst into her mind. She never remembered a man making her so curious and so annoyed at the same time. Or so... unsettled. And should she decide to act on those conflicting emotions and see which one was the most explosive...

Not trusting herself to answer Hank's question, she simply tipped her head in response.

"Has he got a name?"

He's got a lot more than a name. She repeated the cowboy's own words, "Lang Thompson, from north of Phoenix."

Hank twisted his wrinkled cheek, considering, so she asked, "You know him?"

He nodded. "I might. Is his dad Cordes Thompson, the horse breeder?"

"We didn't get into personal questions," she replied, a bit too quickly.

A light red flush crept up the cowhand's neck. "Of course not. Pardon me."

Sorry she'd embarrassed him, she shrugged, hurrying to add, "Anyway, he said it would only take a couple days."

"There's plenty of room in the bunk house. I'll keep an eye on him."

Victoria appreciated his protective attitude. She didn't know what she would've done without him. "Thanks, Hank."

"I'm off to have another try at fixin' that tractor."

She stood up. "Dinner at five."

"Wouldn't miss it." He plunked his hat back onto his bald head, backing away with Promise at his side.

"Hank?" Working hard to keep her tone neutral, she added, "Talk to Mr. Thompson about dinner, please."

"Yes, ma'am."

Victoria checked her watch. There was still plenty of time to finish sorting the tack she'd been digging through before Lang Thompson came crashing into her life.

* * *

From its perch on a fence rail, a cactus wren cocked its head and fixed Lang with a beady-eyed stare. Its brown spots stood out against the late afternoon sunshine while its unblinking eyes watched his every move. He scowled at it but it didn't take the hint to fly away. All he needed now was for that hairy dog to come by and scrutinize him too.

He tossed the last of the broken boards into the bed of his truck and pulled off his leather work gloves. Tearing out the mess had taken longer than he'd expected. A squint-eyed glance at the sun assured him he'd been at the chore for at least three hours.

Mealtime better be soon. That drive-through breakfast he'd eaten at 7:30 wore off about the time he stepped into the shower.

Or maybe that had been an altogether different kind of hunger.

He clamped down on that line of thinking. The shapely rancher had the right moves but he knew what kind of woman she was even if she didn't.

Try as she might to act like an accomplished seductress, Victoria Marana was wife material. She had "marry me" stamped all over her and Lang was not looking for commitment. That route wasn't for him. He wasn't looking for anything except a long stretch of sandy beach, a hot sun to burn away his memories and an endless supply of women. He'd have a different one every night, just to make sure he didn't start preferring one over another. Because wanting only one... that's when a man's trouble started.

He swung into the cab and turned on the ignition. After he dumped the broken boards on the burn pile, he'd come back and take the measurements so he'd know how much siding to buy.

"How's it going?"

Lang poked his head out the window to find the old man strolling toward him, his hands shoved in his coverall pockets, the dog tagging beside him. "I'm on my way to unload the stuff where you told me to."

Hank nodded. "You do that, then come on up to the house for dinner."

Before Lang hit the gas pedal, Hank continued forward, asking. "Miss Marana said you're from around Phoenix. You have a ranch up that way?"

"Used to." He waited, hoping that would be the end of the conversation.

"I like that sayin' 'it's a small world,' because it's true." The hand looped around to head toward the main house. The dog jogged beside him.

29

Lang shrugged off the odd comment. Old timers were known for being eccentric.

The truck hopped up and down as Lang followed the two-track road around behind the bunkhouses. Internal heat trickled through him as he passed Paradise Hideaway. What kind of game was Victoria playing anyway? Why was she pretending to be something she obviously wasn't?

As much as he wanted to shake it off, curiosity stuck to him. Curiosity about her and her plans for The Circle Cat. He hated to admit it, but he was filling up with questions that shouted for answers.

It was easy to see why his cousin insisted he stop by and look the place over. For someone with a solid work ethic and a hefty load of know-how, the ranch had a lot of potential. Lang chuckled. That would leave Victoria Marana out. She'd be running home to daddy soon enough.

He followed the track to its end. An arch of tree stumps and logs for seating surrounded a neat stack of brush. A tight circle of stones separated the sitting area from the burn pile. It was the perfect setting for trail-weary tourists.

Okay, he had to give her some credit. What she'd managed to get done so far impressed him. But she'd get tired of breaking her nails about the same time she realized that animals needed tending regardless of their owner's social obligations.

It didn't make sense for someone like her, a woman who could be living anywhere, to be staying alone out in the middle of the desert. The obvious reason, that she was running away from something, didn't fit. She didn't have the look of a woman running scared. Her face shone with pride and expectation. She was right where she wanted to be. Or so she thought.

What else could there be? She didn't have anything to prove and she sure wasn't going to find a husband out in the middle of nowhere.

He paused and rubbed his hand across the stubble dotting his jaw. Maybe he ought to find a way to convince her that she didn't belong at The Circle Cat. If he did, he could talk her into selling the place to Cole and him.

She'd be better off and him—well, he'd have to start all over again. Maybe that wouldn't be so bad.

Maybe.

As long as he and Cole kept up that bachelor's only policy they'd talked about, then he wouldn't have to worry about losing it all a scheming woman. Again.

Mexico? It would always be there for him when he needed it.

Lang heaved the boards out of the truck bed and tossed them onto the pile. Soon enough, the pile was overflowing and likely to produce some sky-high flames. There wasn't anything nearby to catch fire but the intensity of a fire that big was sure to frighten a city slicker like Victoria.

A grin spread across his face. That'd be a sight to see. The awesome heat of the flames might cook some sense into her.

Not only was she attempting the impossible with the ranch, she was also messing with his head. That silly, sex kitten act on the porch. What was that all about?

He could come right out and ask her what game she was playing. It would be easy enough to point out the striking contrast between her flirtatious ways and how she'd blushed when he'd started to undress in front of her.

He hefted the last board and turned toward the horizon. A hawk soared above him, probably watching a mouse, getting ready to pounce on it. The way Victoria circled around him, he could relate to that mouse.

No, he wouldn't ask her about her game. Why she wanted to play the part of a tease was her business, not his.

He shook his head and chuckled.

Then again...

Maybe if he played along, softened her up, she'd listen to him when he asked her to sell. If they played by his rules, he'd get what he wanted and she'd get what she needed.

A tremor of expectation moved through him. He'd handled women a lot more experienced than that filly. Sure, he had an attraction to her, so he'd have to keep his guard up. As long as he stayed in control he'd be fine.

No problem.

Chapter Four

After an hour of fast work in the tack room, Victoria headed to the kitchen and cleared out the boxes and set the table. The new blue and white floral dishes were perfect, sturdy and functional but pretty. The simple plates and matching glasses were exactly the thing she'd always imagined would be right for a ranch.

She snickered. Her stepmother would hate them.

Hank rolled in, eyed the improved dinner table and then sat at his usual spot across from the window. "We run out of paper plates?"

She grinned at the humor in his voice. "I had to get unpacked sooner or later." Pulling ice from the freezer, she added, "We'll be having guests soon."

"Think we'll be ready on time?"

"Yes," she replied without even considering the possibility that they wouldn't.

She tossed some ice into a tall glass, filled it with tea and set it by his plate.

He nodded his thanks. "I met up with Lang."

"Oh?" She worked at keeping her tone light. "I haven't seen him around." Hank didn't need to know she'd gawked at Lang nonstop while he loaded his truck bed with broken boards. The brawny image of his swaying shoulders had stuck with her ever since and it wasn't likely to fade any time soon. And the way his thighs flexed each time he bent... that picture might never go away. "Did you tell him to come to dinner?"

"Asking about me?"

Victoria shifted to see the object of her wayward thoughts moving through the front room. His lightly colored plaid shirt showed off his sun darkened skin and hinted at the strapping muscles beneath. Funny, she hadn't noticed that cowboy swagger before. Somehow the cocky stride made his legs look even longer.

Lang's new air of self-confidence swirled around her, short circuiting her senses, fraying her nerves. When he laughed at something Hank said, a flash of heated irritation nearly made her scowl but she fought against it. She wasn't going to give him the satisfaction of knowing she even remembered that embarrassing bunkhouse scene.

She swallowed against the tension gathering in her throat and forced some friendly words out. "Hi, Lang. Hank was just telling me you two already met."

Lang nodded at the older man. "Thanks for the help. I found the burn pile." He turned his self-satisfied grin her way. "That's a nice fire pit you have there. Your guests are going to have a real fine time."

He hooked a chair leg with his boot heel, pulling it under him as he sat. Looking like he owned the place, he leaned back.

There was definitely something different about him. Annoyingly different.

The buzzer on the stove went off, making Victoria jump. Glad to have a reason to turn away, she grabbed a pair of oven mitts and pulled the casserole out of the stove. Within a couple minutes, she had it on the table, along with the salad and dinner rolls.

She finally got the nerve to look Lang square in the face. He still had that aggravating grin on his well-shaped mouth. His brown eyes sparked with a dare. Inwardly she fumed. So he was still laughing at her?

Let him.

Victoria was finished letting other people hold her back, telling her what she should and shouldn't do—who she could and couldn't be. If she decided to try out her grab-the-world-with-both-hands personality on Lang Thompson, he'd just better hold tight to that cowboy hat, because she'd knock him flat with her new, improved, sexually advanced self.

"Looks wonderful as usual, Miss Marana. Sit down so we can eat."

Hank's suggestion broke into her jumbled brain, making her realize she'd been standing by the counter like an idiot.

Summoning her enhanced self-confidence and attitude, she nodded at the cowhand then looked at Lang, who lifted one eyebrow the same way he had when he'd caught her staring at him by his truck. Before he could see the blush spreading across her face, she pulled out a chair and glided down.

Hank picked up the casserole, put a serving on his plate and then passed it to Lang. She started the salad and Lang picked up the rolls. The gentle clatter of silverware barely filled the kitchen. Apparently, being talkative was not included in Lang's new persona.

Hank finally broke the quiet. "Where're you headed, Lang?"

Victoria continued eating, peering at Lang from under her lashes. The arrogant expression faded a bit but his voice stayed easy. "Mexico."

The old cowhand pressed for more. "Goin' there on business?"

Lang swallowed some iced tea, shook his head. "Nope."

Hank shrugged and let the topic drop. Victoria turned back to her salad, taking more time than necessary to cut the tomatoes. Leave it to men to clam up when the conversation got interesting.

She could pick up the thread but she didn't want Lang to get the misguided notion she cared where he was headed. He seemed to think he already had in her in his back pocket.

The lull of quiet got her thinking about her plans for the next few days. Her to-do list never grew shorter and the preparations weren't going to take care of themselves. Top on that list was to get some horses. "Hank, you ready to go over to Tombstone with me?"

The old man frowned. "You going tomorrow?"

Victoria nodded, a sense of foreboding settling in her stomach.

Hank avoided her, turning instead to the man across from him. "Lang, you know much about horses?"

A flash of keen interest brightened Lang's gaze, then vanished just as quickly. His eyes narrowed, his expression grew wary. "Why do you ask?"

"I was supposed to take Miss Marana over to the auction in Tombstone, to pick out some horses but, I, um—"

Lang set his fork down. "You asking me to go with her?"

Victoria was stunned silent. Going to the auction had been Hank's suggestion. He'd been *excited* about going. Now he was trying to push her off on a total stranger.

She scowled at him but he wasn't looking her way. He was still waiting for Lang's reply. Like a crusty saloon gambler's, the old man's expression gave nothing away, as he asked, "Could you?"

Victoria's pulse kicked into high gear. Her father and stepmother made a habit of talking around her and she hated it. She opened her mouth to remind them both that The Circle Cat was her place but Lang cut her off.

"I thought I'd get started on the barn."

The strain in Lang's voice piqued her curiosity, so in spite of her frustrations, she kept her mouth shut, and waited.

If Hank was right about Lang coming from a family of horse breeders, that could work in her favor. She needed expert advice. The best dude ranch in Arizona needed the best animals. Selecting hardy trail horses from an open lot couldn't compare to the few well-researched purchases she'd made with her father.

The heavy silence returned, Victoria stubbornly waited it out while she studied her few remaining pieces of lettuce.

Lang sighed. "What kind of horses are you looking for, Victoria?"

So he was interested. In horses anyway. Or in going to Tombstone? "I need a dozen, solid, trail horses."

He shifted his casserole around his plate. "I do need to get the lumber. And those lines I rigged on my truck, well, I need some parts from a garage."

37

Hank shoved his chair back with a jerk and scooped up his dishes. "Thanks, Lang. I feel a whole lot better knowing Miss Marana won't be at that auction alone. You never know what sort of unsavory characters might be hangin' about."

The old man set his plate on the counter and cleared out faster than Victoria had ever seen him move.

"Do you want me to go to Tombstone with you?" Lang asked, once they were alone.

Quiet honesty had replaced the earlier cocky attitude.

When she looked into his level gaze, she noticed tiny flecks of heated gold mixed in with the steady brown. The discovery of yet another contrast intrigued her. Lang Thompson was more than a wandering cowboy.

How much more? She lifted her eyebrows. "What do you know about horses?"

"Enough." He looked away as he added, "I'll need to stop for lumber."

Obviously that was all the answer she was going to get. "Okay," she said, rising to pick up the empty serving dishes, "We'll go together." She'd tried to make it sound fun, like they were two friends planning to spend the day together. But friendly did not describe the way he made her feel. Hot and bothered was a lot more accurate. Oh yes—and annoyed. Can't forget that.

Victoria grabbed some of the empty serving plates and slipped over to the sink.

"You seem a little different tonight, Victoria," Lang said softly, coming up behind her to set his plate on the counter.

His heat pressed into her backside, curled around her waist and settled in her stomach.

If he'd move closer, the hard angle of his hips would press against the soft curve of her hips... she arched her back in hopeful anticipation. When she spoke, her voice came out soft and low, surprising even her. "What do you mean, different."

"Quiet. Reserved."

The way he pronounced reserved, prickled her skin, nearly making her shiver against the warmth of his body. She twisted, asking over her shoulder, "What about you?"

His deep, rumbling chuckle brought back that image of him peeling off his shirt. "What do you mean, what about me?"

Unconsciously, her gaze dropped to his wide chest, her mind filling with questions. If only he hadn't stopped undressing. Then she'd already know what the rest of him looked like. If it would match what her imagination had whipped up. The muscles of his thighs wouldn't be as tanned as his arms but oh, they had to be just as hard and unyielding. How would they feel, pressed against hers? What about his hands, skimming across her calves, gliding higher...

"Does dinner include dessert?" he asked, when her wayward gaze finally found his face again.

Heat flashed across her cheeks. He'd set some kind of trap and she'd walked right in. Again.

"Sure, whatever," she muttered, then turned back around and fumbled with the sink fixtures. "How do you like it, um, your coffee?"

He waited until she looked at him then touched her cheek as he replied. "Hot, untouched and out in the open." His mouth slanted, wicked and welcoming, as he fell back. "I'll wait out on the porch."

Was that warm glow in his gaze was a challenge? That sexy undertone a test?

Absolutely.

That suited her fine. He had a surprise coming because no way was he going to get the best of her again. She could top whatever he dished out.

* * *

Lang let Victoria feel the weight of his stare as she placed the tray of coffee and cookies on the table between them, then lowered herself into the chair.

He picked up a mug. "Hot and untouched," he blew at the steam, "Just the way I like it."

She regarded him with wary eyes, speaking lightly. "I aim to please."

The sharp contrast between her guarded gaze and her flippant words tipped him off that he'd better proceed with caution. Now that he'd made his mind up about trying to get her to sell, well, he was ready to do whatever he had to make it happen. Not that she didn't have good reason to be suspicious but what he had in mind was for her own good.

The last thing he needed was for her to get all riled up. He nearly shivered, remembering Lori Anne's high-pitched shriek. No doubt this pretty piece of woman had a squeal that could make his teeth chatter. He'd better back off for a minute, get Victoria onto easier ground. "Do you have a pasture big enough for those horses you plan on buyin'?"

Her eyebrows shot up and she gave him her full

attention. "It's out behind the corral. Want me to show you?"

Mission accomplished—one distracted woman.

Lang nodded, set his coffee down, then followed her around the side of the house. As they walked along, she scanned the yard, probably making note of whatever jobs she wanted him to do for those home-cooked meals and he tried to stay upwind. Her delicate scent had just enough citrus in it to make his mouth water. Not a good thing, since he kept coming back around to the detrimental notion of using her to quench his thirst.

A sweet thing like her could keep a man busy for hours. Days.

"I know going to the auction will slow your work on the barn," she said as they moved along. "Since I really need someone with a good eye for horses... anyway, um... thanks."

She wasn't exactly gushing her thanks, he noted. Apparently, rich girl Victoria was not happy about putting trust in some down-on-his-luck cowpoke.

Her confidence in his horse sense was well placed but she had no way of knowing he and Cole spent the better part of their teenage years driving from one horse auction to the next. She just expected to get what she wanted, because that was the way her kind of woman was. "Better wait to thank me. I may not find what you need."

"I have a feeling you will," she said breezily before pausing by a pasture fence. "It starts there," she stretched up on tiptoe, giving him another angle to admire her pin-up worthy body and then gestured, "and goes way back, five acres, I think."

Then she swung the conversation way off the path he had planned by asking, "Where were you headed today?"

He steeled himself against her natural delight and the dusting of enthusiasm making her whole face glow. "South." He cast her a dark look to make sure she understood the subject was closed. Judging by the easy, enticing swing of her body, she wasn't getting the message.

"Anywhere in particular?"

Didn't she ever give up? He was supposed to be directing the conversation—and getting what he wanted. Not detailing his personal history for her pleasure. "Just south."

Time to turn the tables and hunt for ammunition he'd need to talk her into selling. He swept aside a strand of her hair, leaned in. "What about you, Victoria? Where do you see yourself in the future?"

"Right here at The Circle Cat," she replied, a slight waver in her soft voice.

He moved in, near enough to feel the womanly heat of her body, close enough to see the cute freckles dotting her nose. "You sure about that? No cowboy on a white horse going to come and take you back to his ranch?"

All hesitation vanished from her face, cool confidence replaced it. "I'm going to stay right here, alone, making this place into a successful business."

Maybe he'd been wrong about her. "By *yourself*," he said, to be sure he understood her meaning.

She leaned back, fixed him with a resolute blue gaze and lifted her chin. "That's right."

No wedding bells rang in her head? Impossible. She was just in denial.

He jumped in with another one he'd been mulling over. "I bet with your dad's money you could have this place fixed up in a hurry. What's the hold up?"

Her chin rose even higher. "Like I said, I'm doing this alone." She said the next statement with a self-assured smile. "That means I'm doing things my way and without help."

My kind of woman.

Damn!

Victoria was not his kind of woman!

Lang nearly bit his tongue off grinding his teeth as he fought against that ridiculous notion. He must have some kind of radar that sought out women who were all wrong for him. "What if things don't work out?"

"They will."

Lang traced the tender curve of her jaw line with his gaze then lifted his hand to follow that same trail with his fingertips. Her skin was smooth, warm and supple, yet her eyes held strength and certainty. She didn't look like a woman who was likely to change her mind about sticking around. This woman had more than her share of fortitude.

He would've liked to respect her for it but she was in his way. And, he added to soothe his conscience, she was doing herself a great disservice.

But it wasn't his conscience that needed the most soothing.

Keep your pants zipped and your hands to yourself, cowboy.

Lang dropped his arm.

He wouldn't bother asking her how she could be so sure things would go her way. Undoubtedly things always had, so in her mind the possibility that they wouldn't didn't even exist. That meant she wasn't anywhere near ready to sell. Not yet, anyway. What she needed was a jolt to push her into reality.

Lucky for them, he was already one step ahead of her. "Have you tried out that bonfire pit yet?"

Because his question came out of the blue, he wasn't surprised by the curl of her eyebrows as she shook her head.

He angled back, putting some distance between them. "It looks great but don't you think you better be sure it works before the guests get here?"

Her cheek twisted as she considered the possibility. "It could *not* work?"

So she wouldn't spot the grin pulling on his mouth, he turned away, pretended to forget about the whole thing.

After a long pause, she tapped him on the arm. "You really think I should try it out?"

He feigned lack of interest with a noncommittal shrug. "Can't hurt."

"Want to come with me?" The question was quiet, the welcome softness in her eyes speaking volumes.

For three, long, heavy beats of his heart, he forgot he'd been baiting her into asking him that very question. Then—he remembered. "Guess so. You got matches?"

"Got some in the kitchen." She called over her shoulder as she trotted toward the house. "I'll meet you there."

He'd be ready, willing and able.

Chapter Five

Within minutes, Victoria stood beside one of the bulky stones that rimmed the inner circle of the bonfire pit. The wide arcs of fat stumps and cut up logs that bordered the pile would seat at least a dozen people.

With only the two of them there, the area looked empty. Instead of giving her room to breathe, the vast desert air created an unnerving intimacy.

Her mind drifted back to Lang. To practical questions about who he was and where he was headed, then to more intriguing ones, like how he kissed. Or made love. Compared to those looking-more-dull-by-the minute business types she'd gone out with in the past, she didn't think he'd hold her at a polite distance the first time—

"Stuff some of that tumbleweed into this pocket and we'll start it here," Lang said, pointing to a wide opening among the busted boards he'd dumped earlier.

"Change your mind?" he challenged, when she didn't jump to do his bidding.

"Of course not."

Not about the fire either.

Satisfaction made her smile when he grabbed a couple handfuls of dry twigs and stuffed them in the hole himself. After he sliced his palm through the air, he turned to her. "Want me to light it?"

45

What she really wanted was to ask him why he'd done that thing with his hand. Was it some sort of test for the air? Or was he chasing away a mosquito? There wasn't any way to ask without looking like an inexperienced ninny, so she dug the matchbook out of her pocket and tore one off.

After she struck it, she tossed it on top of the twigs. Within seconds the flames spread, hopping onto the wide boards. The dry branches spit tiny bits of ash and Victoria had to step back. When she did, she noticed Lang watching her, a strange expression loitering on his rugged face.

Speculation?

The heat from the flames pressed onto her so she stepped over the seating logs. When the orange and red spread and skipped higher, she had to back up again. Within minutes, huge pointed flames stabbed at the sky while boards popped and snapped.

The raw beauty of the fire burned away the frustrations of the day and took her breath away. Its all-consuming energy had a powerful life of its own. Time stalled and she couldn't do anything except stare at the fascinating flames. Suddenly, all the flames blended into one huge wave of fire, forcing her to back up yet again. When she did, she collided with Lang.

He steadied her by cupping his warm palms over her shoulders. "Everything okay?"

"No, it's not okay." She sagged into the internal flames caused by the warmth of his touch and the strength in his hands. "It's fantastic. They're going to love it."

"They're... You... You aren't, um... " His mouth dropped open, his gaze bounced to her neckline.

46

"Too hot?" When his eyes darkened, that inner heat blazed hotter, fizzling all the way down each nerve ending. She tugged on her shirt with quick, jerky motions. "I guess I'll have to move those stumps back or my guests will roast."

In a flash, he frowned, dropped his hands. Without him to protect her from the thin, desert wind the night turned chilly, causing her to shiver. His all-consuming gaze took in every tiny motion and her nipples hardened under his attentive gaze. Tension gripped her shoulders, making her anxious and unsure.

"The... Moving the stumps... that would probably be a good idea," he muttered as he stepped away, his gaze still on her breasts. "Even though not every fire will be this big."

His throat jerked, his hands swung aimlessly by his waist. That constant control... it was fading from his dark eyes.

Sweet Lord, she had *him* flustered.

Quickly warming to the notion of making him uncomfortable, she wiggled experimentally, causing her breasts to bounce as she asked, "Why not?"

Unfortunately the movement had as much effect on her as it did him. Her breasts swelled, aching for his touch.

"This pile... is boards from... the barn... and... stuff from all the clean up you and Hank did. Right?" With stiff movements, he peeled his gaze away from her body as he gestured toward the barn and guest cabins. "Once you get this place in shape you won't have as much to burn."

Desire simmered through Victoria, how she wanted him to look at her again. See that she wanted

47

him. The tight connection pulling them together was making her feel as alive and wild as the fire.

She was sure that if he'd only look at her again, she'd be able to look into his eyes and she'd know what to do next.

Damp heat gathered between her legs and her heart pounded, as she stared at him, waiting for her to turn her way.

Lang stole another sidelong glance at Victoria. The glow of the flames made her dazzling eyes even brighter. With her lips slightly parted and her chest rising sharply with each breath, she looked like Christmas morning and the temptation to touch her was stronger than ever.

The desire to know if her lips would taste sweet and yield to him, burned in his heart. Filled him with a painful need he knew might be eased by lifting the thin fabric of her shirt and losing himself in the full, roundness of her breasts. He'd tug down her bra and take her nipples into his mouth, licking each tight tip until she squirmed, her hips making promises by rocking back and forth.

Then he'd lay her across the warm sand and slide down her jeans. A few kisses and she be yanking down her panties, spreading her legs for him and—damn.

His pulsing erection throbbed against his jeans, making it impossible to think about anything but having her right there, out in the open, under the dusky desert sky.

But he had no business yearning after a woman like her. There would be plenty of uncomplicated sexpots in his future, if he wanted them. Women who knew what they were getting themselves into when they came on to a man who had no need for long-term ties.

Swallowing hard, he pulled himself back to reality.

Victoria had no business staying on at The Circle Cat. If only there was a way he could explain that to her, to persuade her into selling the place to him and Cole. It would be for her own good, save her so much heartache. She didn't need to learn life's lessons the hard way. She'd probably never have to learn them at all.

She was making his task difficult but he wasn't about to give up.

Control. Stay in control.

Just soften her up a tiny bit, get her to see things the right way.

His way.

And without making promises—with his mouth or body—that he had no intention of keeping.

He moved toward the hot flames, making a point of slowly brushing against her. Just a light touch to keep them connected.

When she stepped up beside him, a tentative smile played across her lips but there was nothing hesitant about the motion of her body. Every inch of her cried out for his touch. Her graceful arms, her swollen breasts, her slender waist. And most of all her mouth, warm and inviting.

"What is it, Lang?" she asked, gliding her fingertips across his forearms. "You look like you've got something on your mind."

He stepped back, needing the distance to keep himself from touching her. "This place means a lot to you?"

49

"Sure it does," she nodded, her expression open and trusting, still simmering with untapped heat. "It's everything."

"But why, when you could be doing whatever you want?"

"I need a challenge, a chance to see what I'm made of." She set her hands on her hips and stared ahead. The flames made her hair shine, her skin glow. Tight longing coiled through him as she said on a sigh, "I need something to call my own. I need… " She focused hard on the flames, gathering her own personal strength before adding the next word, "Excitement."

The now familiar churning of his gut reminded him of his own spark of excitement. Before Lori Anne's betrayal stamped it out, that glimmer gave him a reason to get up with the sun. His ranch, his horses, they were everything. Without his animals, Lang had as much purpose as last year's calendar.

He looked away from the strength in Victoria's dazzling eyes. The future he'd designed for himself was gone and all that remained was an uneventful and unchallenging moment by moment existence. Daylight hours that used to be crowded with chores and the satisfaction of a job well done, now crept by with each minute dragging him reluctantly along.

"My working alone surprises you?" Victoria's question sliced through his self-pity.

Weary of the fight, Lang gave up and let the heated emotions twisting through him take control. He forgot about wanting the ranch for himself and turned his gaze back to her, allowing himself a complete and unhurried look. Sweet clear innocence, tenderness and beneath that—the kind of passion that makes a man forget his own name. Everything about her promised to take away the pain in his heart.

At least for a little while.

The shreds of his self-control turned tattered and useless. Without that self-control to hold him in check, his cock was in total control. "You surprise me, Victoria," he said, letting his voice drop low and soft.

He watched, waiting, for that flush to spread up her slender neck but it didn't. Would she pull back if he kissed her? Or would she turn some of that passion he saw in her glittering eyes on him?

Damn, she looked intent—and ready. Tension squeezed him tighter, making his heart pound and his body throb with sexual heat. The need to feel her slender legs wrapped around his waist while he thrust into her, pushing harder and faster until lust swam in her eyes burned through him.

How long had it been since he'd felt so… alive?

How long had it been since he'd really wanted to *be* alive?

Had he *ever* felt this way?

Hot, desperate with the need to pound into a woman but still feeling the need to be gentle.

"I was wondering about something." He wrapped his hand around her rib cage, pulling her close enough to see the delicate lashes shading her eyes. His thigh muscles flexed with expectation, urging him to thrust his hips against her. He held back, afraid he'd scare her off.

Once he had her settled close enough to feel the soft press of her breasts against him, she asked on a sigh, "What is it you want to know?"

She lifted her chin so that her back arched and her

mouth was only a breath away from his. With the side of his thumb he traced the outline of tender bottom lip, pausing to admire the way her eyes widened from his caress. "Did all your boyfriends back home tell you how pretty you are?"

In the silence that followed, her chest rose and fell sharply, drawing his attention again to her tight nipples straining against the soft cotton of her shirt. He took his time admiring the taut peaks, straining to remember why he wasn't dropping down to run his thumb across her delicious breasts.

She wiggled closer, working to nestle herself between his legs, pushing against his pulsing cock.

"Well," he prompted as he raised an eyebrow, "Did they?"

She licked her lips, answering with her gaze on his mouth, "Some of them."

"Did they tell you how sexy you are?" He nuzzled the soft, warm spot just below her ear, whispered across her skin. "How just watching you walk can make a man crazy?"

She shook her head, causing glossy strands to flip across his cheek.

Was the fire getter hotter still or were those flames burning him from the inside?

Needing an answer, he pulled back to brush his lips across hers. Not a kiss but more than enough to send a flash of blood to his already aching erection. The tip of his penis chaffed against his jeans, reminding him of the differences between him and Victoria. And how they each wanted different things from that moment—and from life. "I didn't think so," he growled, easing back, letting himself look into her beautiful eyes.

"What about you, Lang," she asked, a touch of that obvious sex kitten grin curving on her mouth, her fingers skimming playfully across the buttons of his shirt. "Do all the girls tell you how sexy you are?"

The chemistry between them was 100 percent true but that not-nearly-honest, come hither smile… this was all a game to her.

Sweet-talking her was one thing but handing over his heart?

Think with your head.

She parted her lips, then pressed them together, as though unsure of what to do next.

Lang's better sense finally charged through the mire of lust that was sucking him down that trail to Troubleville. He loosened his grip on her shoulder, broke the sexual spell by forcing a laugh.

She jumped away, scowling hard. "What's so funny?"

He leaned back, roaring with mock laughter. "You're a sweet girl, Victoria."

"Sweet?" She spat the word, that hot glitter in her gaze turning to ice.

For good measure, he flashed a cocky grin. "Someday you're going to make someone a good wife."

"Wife?" Her back straightened, jutting her breasts up high. "I told you, I'm not getting married anytime soon."

"I may be just a cowboy," he drawled, tugging his attention away from her tempting curves "But my memory's okay. I remember what you *said* about staying single."

"Good." Sparks flickered into the night behind her, drifting into the sky. "Don't forget it either."

With that departing comment, she spun and marched off with her chin high and her back ramrod straight. And her stiff back only made the sweet sway of her ass all that much finer.

Good work, cowboy.

So much for staying in control. That woman scrambled his brains like no other female he'd had the misfortune to come across. And did things to the rest of his body that threatened to send his good sense packing.

That hot chemistry between them was true, even so, as much as she wanted to deny them, nothing was going to change the facts—they wanted different things from life. Sure he'd been listening to her claims that she wanted freedom and fun, but he didn't believe her. He was sure he knew what was down the road for each of them.

Her—marriage.

Him—bachelorhood.

Long-term commitment was not something he intended to get snarled up in again.

Lang shifted away from the fire. There was hardly any wind, still he'd have to stay until it burned down.

Knowing that the evening chill would catch up with him soon, he went after the jacket he'd left on the porch. After making sure Victoria was nowhere in sight, he crossed through the side yard.

Rich girls.

The world would be better off if they all stayed where they belonged. At the shopping malls and country clubs.

For fun, he tried to imagine his conniving ex

doing what Victoria was doing. He didn't get far. For some reason, he could hardly even remember what Lori Anne looked like. He'd thought she was pretty but were her eyes green or hazel? Why had he married her anyway? Was she fun to be with? Did she stand up to him, the way Victoria did?

"Evenin' Lang," Hank called once he reached the porch steps.

Lang paused, pulled himself upright. How much had Hank seen? It wouldn't do for Victoria's hired hand to see his boss snuggled up with the temporary help.

The old man's expression gave nothing away. "Have a seat."

Lang eased himself into the chair.

Hank glanced at the nearly full cups of coffee on the table. "Seen Miss Marana around?"

"She went inside."

"She comin' back out?"

Fat chance. "I don't think so."

"You two had yourselves a roarin' fire out back."

Lang lifted his jacket. "Yeah, I just came to get my coat. I'll sit out there until it burns down."

The old man fastened him with a direct stare. "This ranch means a lot to her."

Hank folded his arms across his chest, letting his unspoken statement to sink in. Instead of resenting the close scrutiny, Lang appreciated it. Victoria needed someone looking out for her. "I understand."

The old man's voice was smooth but firm. "She's been working non-stop ever since she got out here. Don't let her pretty face fool you, she's a determined lady who knows her mind."

Lang didn't need any reminders about her grit. Too bad it was misplaced. "I noticed." He swept his arms wide. "You two have done all the repairs?"

Hank leaned forward to rub his thighs and nodded. "The Perez's were good folks but they wanted to spend their money on travelin' and seein' their grandkids. They sold to Victoria, moved to Vegas."

"You've only been working with her a couple weeks."

"That's right but I know all I need to know. She's fair and hardworking. I'll be staying on here as long as she'll have me."

Lang pushed aside a twinge of guilt. When he and Cole bought the place from Victoria, they'd keep the man on too. He wouldn't have a problem with their bachelors-only policy.

"You'll help her pick out some good animals at the auction?" Hank asked.

When the place became Lang's, the animals would too. "Of course, it'll be no problem. I know what to look for."

"I thought as much. I knew your father way back. You look like him."

A bittersweet smile flashed across Lang's mouth. "No surprise there. I think everybody in Arizona knew my daddy."

"He was a good man. That's why I trust you with Miss Marana."

Trust.

Lang's conscience kicked him in the shins hard enough to make him wince. It wasn't like he was violating some cowboy code of honor. In fact, he reasoned, he was helping a woman in distress. She didn't know she was in distress but that didn't matter did it?

Hank talked about the old days for a while but Lang's mind was reeling so he couldn't even concentrate enough to ask questions. Something downright horrible had happened. That little slip of a woman had managed to do the unthinkable. She'd shaken loose a couple slats in that fence that was supposed to be protecting his heart. In less than 12 hours.

How had he let that happen? Something about her annoying staying power and doggone resolve got under his skin. If he let himself, he'd admit that he liked her. Enjoyed being near her. And that hot combination of sweet innocence and raw sex appeal? Don't even go there, cowboy.

Not to worry though. The pen around his heart was still there. Stay focused, rancher, stay safe. That feisty blonde was wrong, wrong, wrong and bad news to boot.

"Snore?"

Lang snapped out of meandering thoughts.

Hank smacked him lightly on the shoulder. "You with me? I asked, do you snore?"

Lang pretended he'd been listening all along but he probably didn't even fool the dog. "You a light sleeper, Mr. Cartwright?"

"Call me Hank, son." The man stood up and Promise trotted to the steps. "And no, I ain't a light sleeper. I only wanted to know if I was goin' to be missin' out on some nighttime music." The hand's eyebrows pulled together and his mouth twisted into a knowing grin.

An awkward chuckle rumbled out of Lang. "I'll be down at the bunkhouse as soon as the fire gets low."

"I'll be asleep." The old man worked his way down the steps and said goodnight over his shoulder. The dog followed behind, both of them shuffling and looking bone weary.

As the sun started to slip below the earth, Lang hopped off the porch and strode toward the thick smoke swirling up into the night.

Chapter Six

By 10:30 the next morning, Victoria's nerves were shot. She tried to distract herself by admiring the tall roadside cactuses and the rugged mountains in the distance, somehow the scenery didn't offer the same excitement it had on her first drive out to The Circle Cat. She even went so far as to try to imagine Wyatt Earp and Bat Masterson riding the trails alongside the highway.

The cute trick did nothing to make her forget the hunk of a man seated beside her, the words they'd exchanged, or what she'd been thinking of as an almost kiss. That garbage about her being a "good wife someday"! Just thinking about it made her simmering mad all over again. Mad... and curious. Achingly needy.

If only he'd kept his thoughts to himself and put his mouth on hers. Would his kiss have been gentle like the night air? Or hard and quick like the rivers up in the mountains?

If only he'd kept his thoughts to himself.

Why did every man think a woman's only goal in life was to find a husband? Didn't they realize that some women wanted to have a life of their own? Some fun? An adventure?

Even if she did want to get married—which she did not—she'd eliminated that possibility. So there was no point in even considering the idea—it wouldn't be happening for a long, long time.

Thank goodness Lang had offered to drive. In her mental state all she could manage was to sit, look out the window, pretend to admire the scenery and try not to think about the irritating hunk of man seated beside her.

Peeks at his skillful hands and solid shoulders were out of the question. Those looks would only make her wonder, all over again, what could've happened the night before.

No man had ever made her so hungry with anticipation. She might be strung tight but what happened by the fire didn't seem to be affecting him at all. He sat behind the wheel relaxed and indifferent.

She didn't know whether to be mad or insulted.

The longer they drove along in silence, the stiffer the knots in her shoulders became. She'd probably break into pieces when she finally climbed out of the truck.

"We're almost at the San Pedro River, so we'll be at Tombstone in time for lunch," he said without so much as a glimpse her way.

Victoria glanced at her watch. Had they only been on the road for an hour? The friction gnawing at her nerves made her feel like she'd been confined with Lang half the day.

Yet, she had to find a way past her skittishness. They had to discuss the money she had to spend on horses and exactly what kind she needed. Now was as good a time as any except she couldn't get any words out of her mouth. But she couldn't stand the stiff silence either, so she asked, "Do you want to stop for lunch at a restaurant, or would you rather get something at the auction?"

"I don't need anything fancy. Hot dogs at the lot are fine for me."

His tone touched her already sensitive nerves. Was he implying something? Or was she being paranoid? "I like hot dogs," she challenged with a grin.

He glanced away from the highway and smiled for the first time that day. At her expense.

She pressed back her shoulders. "Doesn't everyone eat hot dogs?"

"Some people eat them more often that others," he responded dryly, a slight tug pulling on the corner of his mouth.

Victoria struggled to keep the light in her eyes. He was trying to get at something but what? Big deal if she hadn't eaten a hot dog in years. What did that have to do with anything?

Then it dawned on her. She'd read his attitude all wrong. He'd noticed that two-way attraction but for some stupid reason, he was trying to find something to wedge between them.

Why?

She sat in thoughtful quiet during their stops at the lumberyard and garage. By the time they pulled into the Cochise County Auction lot, her neck was sore and her mouth was worn out from all the frowning.

Anxious to be out in the open again, she pushed the door open, swung out and stepped around to the front of the truck. One look around and her aches were forgotten.

It was fantastic. Dusty cowboys and chattering families swarmed all around, their shouts and calls filling the air with energy. Herds of horses waited in corrals and even more were being unloaded from trailers.

Lang lumbered over. "I'm starving. Let's get

something to eat, then check the horses over. Okay with you?"

Overcome by the thrill of the marvelous chaos, Victoria spun on her heels, admiring it all.

"You ever been to an auction before?" he asked, past her shoulder at a couple of paint ponies tied to a railing under a cluster of trees.

"No! I could kick myself. I can't believe I never took the time. This is incredible. I've never seen so many horses for sale in one place."

He tipped his head, his face tight and expressionless as he pulled his gaze off the animals. "There's a lot of them, that's for sure."

What a grouch. But she wasn't going to let him ruin her fun. "I guess it's no big deal to you. I love it."

"It's the perfect place to buy horses," he muttered vaguely as he made a point of shrugging his strong shoulders, "If you know what you're doing."

So that was it.

He wanted to give her a hard time about needing his knowledge and experience. Victoria opened her mouth to tell him she'd had enough of him entertaining himself at her expense but the quip stuck in her throat, the slight crinkle at the corners of his eyes making her reconsider.

He was teasing her? The sparkle in his brown eyes, insisted he was.

Lordy. The wandering cowboy full of surprises.

The next thing she knew, he was grabbing her arm. "Come on, I'm hungry," he grumbled, pulling her across the gravel parking lot.

When he turned toward the food, his knee brushed against thigh, instantly sparking a series of heart pounding pulses that melted her nerve endings and made her stomach quiver.

Why did someone she'd only met the day before have such an effect on her? It didn't make sense.

She turned and caught his eye. Liquid electricity passed between them but he dropped her arm and took a wide step to the right. They were total strangers and Lang obviously wanted to keep things that way. Otherwise, the night before he would've gone ahead and kissed her and then…

"One or two times?"

Victoria swallowed hard and stared wide-eyed at Lang.

He chuckled at her stunned expression. "I thought men were supposed to be the poor listeners."

"I was listening!"

"Sure, to yourself think." He laughed louder. "Forget it, I was ribbing you about eating hot dogs, like the regular people."

His tone was light, his eyes shining. Still she didn't quite trust him. "I'm a regular person," she said, tucking her chin in and wrinkling her nose.

He smirked. Did he think she was some kind of snob? Where had he gotten that idea?

Oh.

Her father's reputation.

If that was the case, he was all wrong. She'd left all that behind.

Gladly.

No way was she going to spend her afternoons sitting around the club, planning boring luncheons and business dinners like her sister and stepmother. She had her own life to live and she intended to do it. If

Lang thought she was like those boring socialites she'd gone to school with, there had to be some way to show him she was a regular person, an ordinary girl.

Then maybe he'd come around to her way of thinking—a no-strings-attached good time.

After he ordered their food and drinks, she reached in her pocket for some money. He pushed her hand aside. "My treat, princess."

She opened her mouth to protest but his dark scowl stopped her. There was no point in arguing over a couple dollars, so she waited while he paid and then strolled alongside him as he carried the cardboard tray to one of the nearby picnic tables.

The eating area was crowded but Lang found them a spot between a group of teenagers and a noisy family. After Victoria slid in beside him, he set one of the hot dogs in front of her.

Grinning, she dug through the condiments he'd grabbed for two of the mustard packets.

Lang watched in disbelief as Victoria squirted both packets onto her hot dog, then took very huge and most unladylike bite. A bright smudge of mustard stuck to her lip.

How was it that she constantly found a way to surprise him? "No ketchup or relish? Just mustard? What's that all about?"

A devilish twinkle flashed in her eyes but whatever she said was muffled by the mouthful of food. The mischievous bend of her mouth held a challenge his masculine pride wouldn't let him ignore.

He grabbed the remaining mustard packets, three ketchup and two relish packets. With a quick and practiced hand, he dumped all the condiments onto his hot dog, then turned to make a big display out of taking the first enormous bite.

She chuckled, reaching up to wipe the mustard from her lip. He had a hard time chewing because of the laughter rumbling in his chest. Still he managed to make short work of the hot dog. Two bites later it was history.

"Lang Thompson?"

Still chewing like a cow, Lang turned to find a long-time friend of Cole's, rodeo star Vince Haynes. Lang grabbed a napkin to wipe his mouth, scrambled off the picnic bench to stand up and stretched out his hand.

After a huge swallow, he managed to speak. "Hey Vince, what're you doing down this way?"

"I might ask you the same thing," the other man replied as he accepted Lang's hand, shaking it firmly, the crisp white of his sleeve flashing in the bright afternoon sun. His cousin's friend wasn't looking at him though, the man's appreciative gaze was zigzagging across Victoria's calendar girl body.

After Vince let go of his hand, Lang stepped closer to Victoria, looming over her protectively. Even though he would've rather punched the man in the face for staring at her like that, he went ahead and did the socially acceptable thing, introduced them.

Lang wanted to push Victoria back down when she started to rise. He wasn't her keeper, he reminded himself. If she wanted to show herself off, who was he to stop her?

Cole always went on about what a rough and ready stud Vince was and how he always got more girls when they hung around together. Flashy men were probably right up Victoria's alley.

65

Lang scowled while the two of them babbled on—about the weather of all things—like old friends.

Or, two strangers who wanted to be friends.

When he got sick and tired of Vince's boyish grin and exaggerated Texas drawl, he leaned over and cut into their banter. "Miss Marana is here to get some trail horses for her ranch. I came along to make sure she gets some good animals."

Vince managed to pull his attention away from Victoria. "You'll want to get on over to the north corner of the lot then. I came from that way and there's a whole herd getting unloaded." Vince's white teeth flashed. "I'm here looking for a pony for my niece, else I'd be considering them myself."

"Your niece!" the delight in Victoria's voice was as clear as Vince's leering grin was wide. "My sister just got married and I'm already waiting for nieces and nephews. The little girl must be thrilled."

Vince stuffed his hands into his too-tight pants and shifted his polished snakeskin boots. "She will be, she's just a babe now."

Victoria giggled with the other man and Lang suddenly found himself out of the loop. What was so funny about a baby too young to be excited about a pony?

Vince jerked a thumb over his square shoulder. "Lang, why don't you go on over and check out those new arrivals in the corner lot, while I sit with Victoria for a spell?" He nodded at the table. "Looks like you already finished your food."

Lang glanced at the picnic table, taking in the evidence of his three bite hot dog. The twisted condiment packets lay in a heap.

He didn't want to leave Victoria with that so-called stud. So what if his cousin was friends with the guy. Lang didn't know anything about him. Except that all the women thought he was a hottie. That wasn't enough. He could be a crazed lunatic. The next cowgirl killer.

There had to be a way to keep Victoria from staying with Vince.

Lang wasn't being possessive.

Only safe. Reasonable.

Unfortunately, Victoria spoke up too quickly for him to put a stop to things.

"That's a great idea." She gave him a one-handed push and sat her too-pretty-for-her-own-good self on the bench.

Lang was amazed that Vince's painted on pants didn't snap him in two when he eased himself down right next to Victoria. Inches away from her. And that stupid boyish grin was back.

Lang embarrassed himself by childishly shoving his hands in his pockets and kicking at the dirt, making clods of dirt land near Vince's boots.

"Go on, Lang." Vince's expensive watch blinked in the sunlight as he waved him off. "I'll take care of things here."

That's what he was afraid of. He flashed a murderous glare in the grinning cowboy's direction but hottie Vince didn't notice.

"Don't you want to come with me?" Lang asked Victoria, annoyed at the plea in his voice.

"No, you go take a look," she replied over her shoulder. "I'll meet you by the truck in 40 minutes. Okay?"

67

With that said, she turned back to the other man asking if he had any photographs of his niece. With well rehearsed movements, Vince slid his wallet out and unraveled a long, plastic strip of baby pictures. He probably had colored condoms in there too.

Thoroughly disgusted with the jealousy tearing at his insides, Lang swung around and stalked off to get involved in the only thing he'd ever been really good at. Dealing with horses.

Chapter Seven

With his back slanted against the hood of her truck, hat tipped low and scuffed boots buried in the dust, Lang looked like all the other cowboys milling about the auction, with one not so small difference. Victoria wanted him to be *her* cowboy.

It didn't make sense, it didn't fit into her plans and considering the information she'd just pried out of Vince, it wasn't going to happen.

According to Vince, Lang had a battered heart he planned to keep locked up until he was "pushin' up bluebonnets". And—according to what Cole, Lang's cousin, told Vince—Lang had sworn off women.

All women.

For good.

Still, she paused to hitch up the box in her arms and soak in the heady rush she got simply by looking at Lang. That giddiness was hers, the memories of how it felt to tingle from head to toe would be something she'd keep long after he left.

About the time she reached the truck, he turned, meeting her gaze. His focus dropped quickly to the box in her arms. A little something, somethings—actually, she'd picked up to brighten up the ranch.

Swimming through the crush the of excitement

that grew harder to control each time she came near Lang, or even thought about him, she stepped up and opened the box. "Aren't they sweet?"

"Chicks?" Disbelief hung on his voice, his gaze trailing the wobbly birds as they tottered around the box.

No way was she going to let him ruin her fun. "Think of the great time the kids'll have hunting for eggs. The girls assured me they'll be good layers."

"Girls?"

She sighed, tipping her head toward the row of trucks next to the concession area. "The girls I bought them from."

"Of course." He pushed away from the truck and angled his hat back, drawing Victoria's attention to the overlong locks brushing against his corded neck. "What kind of chickens are they?"

She ignored the mocking tone in his voice, replying brusquely, "The egg laying kind."

"You don't know what kind they are, do you?" he challenged. "I bet you didn't even ask."

"No, I didn't ask." She closed the top, carefully tucking in the edges. "They'll lay fresh eggs for my guests. That's all I need to know."

"All I know is that I shouldn't leave you alone anymore." As soon as the words were out, he scowled even harder, if that were possible and gently took the box from her. "You're all set with the horses," he said, sliding the box of chicks into the shade under the truck.

"You found some?"

"Vince has a decent eye," he grumbled, then spun and stalked off, asking her to follow over his sturdy shoulder.

Victoria jogged after him, calling, "We need to talk."

"No, we have to get over there now." He slowed just long enough for her to reach his side. "I told the seller we'd be by within a half hour."

It was her turn to scowl. "You made a deal without me?"

"Don't get yourself in a snit." He flashed her an annoying know-it-all grin and gave her a gentle push on the small of her back. Warmth spread across her as they moved together, him speaking. "I know horses. These are the animals you need. If we wait too long, he's going to put them in the auction, then we'll never get them together. You don't want that to happen.

"These animals already know each other, that'll make a big difference out on the trail. Especially since you're going to want to use them right away."

It would be so easy to let him take matters into his capable hands but she wanted to do everything on her own. That had been the plan, anyway. So why was she enjoying his take-charge attitude?

As they approached the north corner, she pushed that question aside and grabbed his arm, tugging against his powerful stride. "Lang, we really have to talk about the horses."

A grimace creased his face but he stopped, giving her his full attention. "Okay. What do you want to know?"

"I need to know how much they cost."

He studied her, contemplation clouding his eyes. "Why? Don't you think I'll get you a good deal?"

"It's not that." When his gaze softened, she went on. "Remember, I'm doing this on my own. I don't have an unlimited supply of money, even though you seem to think so."

He rubbed his jaw, doubtful, yet considering. "Okay, how about this. You tell me how much you have to spend, how many horses you want, then let me do the talking."

Victoria didn't like turning things over like that. She'd left Phoenix to get away from depending on people but without the best horses…

He tapped his boot impatiently, a grin appearing on his mouth. She swatted his arm, lingering just long enough to enjoy the heat of his skin. "Stop laughing at me."

"I'm not laughing." He tipped his head, looking at her between his thick, silky lashes. "Did you hear me make any sounds?"

Tiny lines crinkled around his dark eyes.

Folding her arms, she grumbled, "I'm glad you find this so funny."

A seductive glimmer flashed through his gaze. "Poor little rich girl needs help from some wandering cowboy, now why would I find that funny?"

She snickered in spite of his light-hearted barb. "Put that way, it does sound pathetic."

The chuckle finally rumbled out of him. "Now who's being nasty?"

"Okay, you get your way." She told him how much she had to spend.

"How many horses?"

"Twelve."

She waited, all he did was nod his handsome head.

"I know that's not much money—"

He cut her off with his hand, set his hand at her waist and started walking again. "You're not looking for show animals, Victoria. Bloodlines don't matter here. You're only after reliable, sure footed mounts."

Expectation danced inside her, side stepping his request that she keep quiet. "You think I have enough?"

"I'll take care of it. Remember, no talking. I make the deal." He fixed her with a searching stare. "You know, it's okay to accept help from people."

"I guess," she replied. But because she didn't agree and she was getting tired of the way he kept disregarding her opinions and having a laugh at her expense, she added, "But I need to learn how to do these sorts of things myself."

He rolled his eyes. "A woman like you is never alone for long. Some man will happen by."

A woman like you... some man...

Color splashed across her cheeks and iron settled in her spine. "Do you have a problem understanding basic concepts, Mr. Thompson?"

He blinked in surprise then scanned her face, looking for a clue.

"I'm not waiting for some man to happen by and... " Frustration steamed inside Victoria, forcing her to blurt out the truth. "*Even* if I wanted to, I can't get married."

His back straightened as he grabbed her elbow and pulled her aside, away from the main line of foot traffic. "What do you mean... can't?"

Victoria stumbled to a stop then sucked in a quick breath as the dark gaze of his eyes burned into her soul. The hard pull of his mouth, the steady, firm grip on her arm...

"You're already married? But you said… "

How predictable.

She should've seen it coming.

Jerking her arm away, she said, "No, Lang. What I mean is that I can't get married because I cashed in my wedding fund to buy The Circle Cat."

After a pause, he spoke again, his whispered words framed with cynicism. "Wedding fund?"

"That's right." She squared her shoulders, set her fists on her hips. "See, so I don't have any money left for—"

"Your *wedding* was going to cost the same as a ranch?"

"I didn't want one of those huge designer weddings anyway. And I don't want to get married without having a life of my own first. I want to have fun, on my own terms. Not tie myself to someone who's going to boss me around and tell me what to think. I had a choice to make, so I did. What's the big deal?"

His gaze turned steadily blacker until a chill shot straight to her toes. She blinked, her boldness deteriorating under his stare.

Lang watched Victoria press her sweet lips together, looking lost and confused. Emotions galloped through him, none he wanted to give names to. If the first had been jealousy, at the thought of her belonging to someone else, that had been quickly replaced by resentment—and a host of other downright ugly sentiments.

If he'd been dense enough to need a guarantee that this woman wasn't fit for the life she was trying to squeeze herself into, that was it. She didn't belong at

The Circle Cat any more than he belonged in a fancy high rise office.

He had to find the way and make the ranch his.

The sooner they got the horses in the trailer, the better. Putting his concerns back where they belonged—on the horse deal—he asked, "You think you can keep quiet for ten minutes, while I settle up with the seller?"

Her vibrant blue eyes sparked with irritation while she considered her options. "Yes, I already agreed to that. I won't say a word."

He swept his arm behind her, guiding her back onto the path that led to the back lot. He wasn't being possessive. He was simply being efficient, helping her get through the crowd.

A wedding fund?

Who ever heard of such a thing?

And who spent that much money on a party?

Rich girls, that's who.

Girls who didn't belong out in the desert alone.

After they pulled up near the seller's spot, he pointed to a tall wooden post. "You wait here, I'll go find the seller."

She scowled but did as he asked.

Within minutes, he'd made the deal and taken care of arrangements to have all but four of the animals delivered. When he got back to Victoria he pulled her away from the post with a curt, "Deal's done. We take four with us now, they'll deliver the rest later this afternoon, after the auction closes. Come on, let's go get your trailer."

Her eyebrows pulled together as she dug her heels in. "I want to see them first."

That stubborn side again. If it weren't so annoying he'd admire her for it.

Leading her across the aisle, he pointed to a glossy palomino with a mane that matched her own golden locks. "See her?"

Victoria reached up to scratch under the horse's blonde forelock. "Hey there, beautiful."

"Like her?"

The horse blinked its long lashes and stepped closer, Victoria stretched up to scratch under the mane. The clingy fabric of her shirt pulled even tighter and Lang's gaze fell to the swells of her breasts. Just two layers of fabric, then glorious bare skin. Sweet tight nipples, heat and soft flesh.

He tried to turn away, then she leaned to the side, making her breasts sway and her shirt slide up enough to give him a peek of that smooth, creamy, yielding…

Damn.

He clenched his fists in a pointless attempt to squelch the desire flickering in his veins, swelling his cock instantly. Not even a look-but-don't-touch policy was enough where she was concerned.

Sure, he'd seen plenty of pretty women in his day but Victoria—well, she wasn't like a single one of the others.

Of its own accord, his gaze skimmed over her taut, flexed body as she petted the horse. Her shirt rose up again and he had to grit his teeth to keep from tipping his head down to peek up inside.

Put your hands down, Victoria.

If she kept that up, he'd pull her into an empty stall and sweet talk her into sliding down her pants while he tugged down his jeans.

Would she go along with it?

He blinked, who was he kidding?

All her attention was on the animal in front of her.

In an attempt to trick his cock into forgetting she existed, he forced his gaze down, only to end up spotting the thin band of her lavender lace panties peeking above her jeans.

He swallowed and tried to think of something very un-sexy.

Like mucking out stalls.

Stalls filled with hay, soft enough to lie on.

With Victoria, naked and panting beneath him.

"So. Do you like her?" he barked, staring at the wooden post beside her.

"Like this horse?" Oblivious to his painful arousal, she dropped her arms to rest her hands on the metal rail. "She's beautiful, gentle and so sweet."

"Good. She's yours."

"This one?" she pointed to the quiet mare she'd been petting. The ecstatic expression she flashed his way pulled hard on that fence he was desperately trying to keep around his emotions.

"Her name's Sasabe," he grumbled. "That black pony, chestnut and paint with her, they're in the deal too."

He never would've thought she'd get so excited about something that didn't come in one of those glossy shopping bags. Arching across the aisle toward eight other beautiful horses, he said, "The others are in a corral across the way."

Her anger from the moment before forgotten, she threw her arms around him, hugging tight and beaming. "Thanks, Lang."

While Lang reluctantly enjoyed Victoria's sassy comebacks and stubborn insistence, her soft words of thanks almost made his knees buckle. He didn't want her looking at him like that, all gentle and vulnerable. If she kept gazing at him that way there was no telling what he'd do. Like forget how bad a broken heart felt for starters.

Then he'd start thinking about her delicate hipbones pressing against his most sensitive body parts and the tender, welcoming scent that clung to her skin and how badly he was starting to think if he ever got hold of her he might never let go.

His sexual thoughts about her were a bother but that line of thinking was dangerous.

The sooner they got the animals loaded, the sooner they'd be back at the ranch and he'd be able to get away from her. At least long enough to hammer down on his raging male hormones.

Lang dropped his arm to her waist, guiding her back in the direction of the parking lot. He strode as fast as he could. Victoria, with her long legs, matched him step for step. They rounded the corner of a beat-up SUV filled with screaming girls and Lang pulled her close when a burly man started up its engine.

What happened to his plan of keeping his hands to himself? Anxious to correct his mistake, he dropped his arm to dig through his pocket for the truck keys.

"Did you want to stop anywhere on the way home?" he asked, unlocking the door.

"No, I want to get those horses home and settled," she replied over the chicks who'd started peeping when she picked up the box. "Then I've got to finish cleaning out the guest houses."

Lang wanted to stay disgusted with Victoria but it was difficult with her holding that crazy box in her arms while her face read all business. She looked sweetly ridiculous—not at all like a pampered socialite who was dead set on running a ranch.

A question struck him and he wondered why he hadn't asked it already. Since he was more convinced than ever he had to find a way to get her to sell to him, it was something that mattered. "Do you already have guests scheduled for next week?"

"I sure do."

"Aren't you cutting it a little close?" he asked over the hood before climbing into the cab to reach over and open her door. Once she was inside, he continued, "Maybe you should postpone them, you know, give yourself more time to get the place up and running."

She settled the noisy box on her lap, set her arms across it, crossing them at the wrists. "That really isn't an option."

Limited options were something he knew all about. Like when your wife finds a richer cowboy, runs off with him and then you lose everything you have fighting to keep what you'd started out with in the first place.

Lang grumbled as he carefully drove the truck and trailer down the two track which ran alongside the perimeter of the auction lot then continued around to the back, trying with very little success to concentrate on maneuvering safely. Even though it took 40 minutes finish the deal, load Sasabe and the other three, he was still fighting the foul mood brought on by Victoria's confession about her absurd wedding fund. It wasn't her fault her daddy had money, still, just the notion…

"You've done this auction stuff before haven't you?" she asked, cutting into the dark cloud muddling his brain.

"Once or twice." If he told her the truth, that he and Cole had spent every weekend all summer driving from auction to auction, she'd probably think that was a real hoot. The men she knew probably spent their time on the golf course or reading the *New York Times*.

"You got me a really good deal," she said.

Yeah. He did.

Why couldn't she let it go? "He wanted to sell them all together. We wanted to buy them that way. It worked out."

His conscience popped up again, reminding him that if things went his way, the horses she was so excited about wouldn't be hers for long. But they'd be part of the ranch and she'd get her money back if she sold to Cole and him—correction *when*.

Except he'd make her take Sasabe. He wouldn't want any blonde horses hanging around the place reminding him of her.

As they approached the turn off to get back onto the highway, an odd clanking came from the trailer.

Something loose?

Lang angled the truck off to the side of the wide road and slowed to a stop. "I need to double check the latches, make sure the horses are secure." He grumbled to himself, then added, "I've been… distracted… and I don't want animals getting hurt because of my stupidity."

Instead of staying put the way she should've,

Victoria slid out of the cab and met him at the back of the truck. As he moved from one side to the other, checking each inch of the trailer, she followed along staring at him the whole time.

Why did he have to notice every little thing about her? Her scent, her voice—her mere presence—was enough to distract him all over again, making it harder and harder to focus on the safety of the animals.

His tolerance was wearing thin.

She was still bubbling with enthusiasm.

"You're really good at this sort of stuff," she said, bending lower to get a better view of the latches he was double checking.

"As you pointed out," he said with a controlled snarl, "I've done it before."

Victoria's patience snapped. "I don't know what your problem is, Lang Thompson. You've got no right to take it out on me. I didn't dig you out from under some rock. You're the one who smashed into my life and messed up my plans."

"Your plans?" He straightened, glaring down at her. "Just what are your plans, Victoria?"

"What a stupid question." Refusing to let him intimidate her with his size, she stepped forward and went toe to toe. "You know exactly what I'm trying to do."

His blistering stare flickered over her face and settled on her mouth. Incredible quivering flowed through Victoria and she swallowed hard against the tightness in her throat, had to try harder to breathe. Heat pooled in her stomach, spiraled out with each heavy beat of her heart, each pulled breath.

For a crazy, wonderful second, she was sure he was going to kiss her. But he didn't. Instead, he whispered, "What was it you said? You're going to have fun? An adventure on your own terms?"

The contemptuous tone in his voice chaffed her already frayed nerves. Of course he focused in on that part, rather than the part about seeing what she's made of—of proving that she could make something of herself. "Why do you find that so hard to believe?"

"You don't strike me as the kind of girl who has *that* kind of fun," he remarked, still leaning in close enough to press his lips to hers.

"Spit it out, Lang." She inched closer, lifting her chin, unwilling to give him the satisfaction of her backing down. "What kind of fun?" she taunted.

"Short-term flings, one-night stands, quickies in the back of some guy's truck," he clarified with a sneer that didn't match the glowing heat in his gaze.

Thick longing curled through her, silencing any snappy comeback she might've been able to think up and giving him time to continue with his idiocy.

"You were practically drooling all over Vince," he stammered, backing up, waving his hands, "But I bet you didn't give him your number because you knew he'd just use you to add another notch in his saddle."

Vince?

Was he serious?

How blind could Lang be?

She'd been practically drooling all over *him,* he'd been too disinterested to care, let alone notice. Victoria's simmering blood rolled to a boil. "You think I should try it, huh? One night stands? Quickies?"

"Forget it, Victoria. Like I said, you aren't that kind of girl."

Victoria took in the arrogant angle of his brows and frowned.

Yet another man, assuming he knew her, understood her and was even telling her how to act. "That's, that's… just plain stupid," she sputtered.

Disbelief settled in his eyes and his mouth twitched. "*That's stupid?* That's the best you can do?"

So now he was challenging her?

She'd let him set the pace for way too long.

Fueled by the desire to prove him wrong, Victoria swept forward and wrapped her arms around his neck. Without giving herself time to rethink her hasty actions, she arched up and laid her mouth across his.

Passion, instant and fierce, ignited within her when he wrapped his arms around her and kissed her back. Liquid want coursed through her veins as her body willingly responded to the powerful muscles of his chest, the soft tender caress of his lips, the possibilities of his strong very male body.

Absorbed by his sheer power, the smell of horses, leather and swirling dust, she let herself, tipping her head back, inviting him to deepen the kiss.

When he answered her unspoken request, awareness spread through her—he was as deliciously lost as she was. She could feel it in the eager way his hands tugged at her waist, the hungry way his mouth moved across hers.

When she gasped with satisfaction, he lifted his head. Enjoying the stunned surprise in his needy gaze and the enthusiastic hammering of her own heart, she held on tightly to his shoulders, pressing her hips closer and rocking gently against the swell of his hard penis.

Just when she was about to pull him down for another kiss, a car rolled past with two teenagers hanging out the windows, shouting and whistling loud enough to be heard all the way back at The Circle Cat.

"See?" she said, smiling as she stepped back, flushed from the fantastic sensation. "That was fun."

Lang avoided looking at her. "Get in the truck, I'll take care of the latches."

Chapter Eight

Victoria soon discovered her triumph came with a cost. That simmering sexual heat hadn't gone away as quickly as it'd come on. In fact, it hadn't gone away at all.

The more she thought about Lang's skillful hands and mind-blowing kisses the worse her distracted stupor got. The ride home had been so excruciatingly long and quiet, she nearly sighed with relief when the turn off for The Circle Cat came into view.

The relief was short lived.

"You've got some visitors," Lang said, steering the truck along the gravel drive. "From the looks of that car, I don't think it's anyone coming about that ad."

Victoria's whole body filled with distress as she blinked, wishing the apparition before her could be part of a dream. Even a nightmare would be better than the truth.

Susie's newly restored Mustang ragtop filled the center of her driveway.

"Know who it is?" Lang asked.

"My dad and stepmother," she replied, barely able to keep the dread out of her voice.

"Isn't that nice." He rolled to a stop, put the truck in park. "Your daddy came to see how things are going."

Victoria glanced at Lang, trying to read his

expression. There was no desire, yet no resentment either. Just plain perceptive steadiness.

She turned her attention back to the very flashy and very unwelcome car loitering in her driveway. Thinking her father had only come to see how things were going would be the understatement of the year. "He's here to snoop around and try to talk me out of this."

One side of Lang's mouth curved up. "Can you be talked out of things?"

She sighed. "That's not the point."

After Lang switched off the engine, he shifted so one arm lay across the bench. "What *is* the point? Everything okay?"

She pulled in a deep breath and smoothed her hair into place, considering. Why was it that simply knowing her father was nearby made her feel like a 12-year-old?

She was a grown woman with a business of her own, not some kid with a lemonade stand. Her father had to accept that sooner or later.

"Everything isn't okay," Lang said when she didn't respond.

"It's not that." She rolled her eyes. "I don't need him poking around while I'm still getting things together that's all. He has a way of making me… "

"Insecure?" Lang supplied, filling in her silence.

There wasn't much point in denying it. "Yes." She blew out a frustrated breath. "I know I shouldn't let him."

"I get it. Parents have a powerful effect on us, even when they're not around."

She was shocked by the depth of Lang's

understanding. The sympathy on his face convinced her that he really did know how she felt. He probably came from a close knit family. Maybe that was why his divorce from Lori Anne had sent him on the one-way road trip to Mexico.

He swung his door open. "You go on up to the house and say hello, I'll unload the horses."

When she climbed out, she spotted Hank and Promise jogging toward them. Even with the threat of her father waiting in the wings, she mustered up a smile. "Wait 'til you see the horses we got. Eight more are being delivered later tonight."

Hank shifted his path toward the back of the trailer. "Got some nice ones?" He climbed onto the sideboard and peeked in. "Victoria Marana! Look at these beauties." He sounded like a six-year-old who'd been let loose on the county fair midway. "That Palomino is fit to be framed."

Victoria pushed her door shut and backed away from the truck. "They're sturdy and strong, exactly what we need. And," she paused when Lang came around the back corner of the trailer, "they all came from the same buyer, so they're already used to working together."

Smug satisfaction creased the old man's face. "I knew Lang would take care of things."

"How do you know I didn't make the deal?" she asked, tipping back her shoulders.

When Hank's mouth dropped, Victoria put her hand on his arm. "That's okay Hank, I'm teasing. I couldn't have done it without Lang. He took care of everything."

Everything that had to do with horses, anyway.

87

Lang stepped between them, seeming uneasy with their compliments. "Hank and I'll manage here. Victoria, you go to the house before your dad comes looking for you."

Good idea. She didn't want her dad and stepmother wandering around the ranch nosing into every little thing. Before she knew it, her dad would have one of his clipboards out and be making a mile-long list of all the things wrong with her place.

As she stepped away, she heard Hank's eager offer to help get the animals settled. Lang wouldn't have been able to get rid of the man if he tried to chase him off with a pitchfork.

The two of them would be busy for a while. If she worked fast, she could get the visit over with and have her dad and Susie back on their way to Phoenix before dinner.

She frowned.

Kicking them out that quickly would be rude. She'd have to invite them to stay through dinner. Eating a meal with her dad and her stepmom sounded like about as much fun as mucking out stalls. No, mucking out stalls would be more fun. She wouldn't have to explain herself to the animals.

The light feminine sound of her stepmother's voice greeted Victoria even before she reached the house. She found her dad and Susie snuggled up on the swing, smiling and looking as though they had all the time in the world to visit. And get in her way.

Victoria took a deep breath, willing herself to relax but ended up blowing it out in frustration. She wouldn't be at ease until the taillights of that bright red sports car glowed as they headed away from the ranch.

As soon as he spotted her, her father rushed over to squeeze her into one of his famous bear hugs. "Sweetheart, I've missed you."

She returned the embrace with a sincere one of her own. "I missed you too, Daddy." Then she peeked around her father's thick shoulder, "Hi Susie, it's good to see you."

Her stepmother flashed her long, coral nails. "It's good to see you too, sweetie. We've been having a nice time chatting with Mr. Cartwright."

Her father eased back, studying her with his deep brown eyes. "You look well enough but from what Hank tells us, you've been working day and night to get this place up to code. And you still have a long list of things that need repair."

"I told you there was a lot to get done," she replied, trying to keep the defensiveness out of her voice.

"Well, I know. I'd assumed you meant things like selecting wallpaper and light fixtures. I had no idea you'd be mending fences and hauling trash."

"It's not bad. I've been having fun."

Susie shook her head. "Really, Victoria you should let your father send one of his crews out to do the heavy work."

"I'm doing fine," she said as gently but firmly, as possible. "I have to be ready on time, I've already got a group of guests scheduled."

Her father stuffed his big hands into his pockets, his head swiveling as he scanned the yard. "This place isn't near ready for folks."

No kidding.

"I know, that's why I've been—"

"—working yourself to the bone?" her father cut in, his frown emphasizing his disapproval.

Before Victoria could redirect the conversation, Susie asked, "Have they seen any pictures? How did you convince them to come?"

Victoria's sigh slipped out but she managed to not roll her eyes. "I put an ad on one of those Internet lists, offering a special rate. A travel agency in California got in touch with me and set everything up."

"An Internet ad? I never would've thought that would work." Her father's mouth twisted, then he shrugged. "Okay then, you going to show us around?"

Victoria breathed an inward sigh of relief. At least they hadn't been snooping around on their own. If she guided the tour, she could skip the real problem areas.

"You go on ahead, Sam." Susie patted her hair and leaned into the floral cushions on the swing. "I'll stay here and put my feet up."

Her father moved to plant a soft kiss on his wife's cheek. "All right, darling. I'll see you when we get back."

Even though Victoria wasn't too crazy about her stepmother, she appreciated the real affection the two of them shared. They had that special kind of devotion some couples envied and permanently single people didn't believe in.

Her father loved Susie and that was all the reason Victoria needed to care for the woman as well. As for really liking her, that was a different story. The two of them would never be on the same page. Or maybe even in the same book.

Her father climbed down the steps. "Okay honey, I'm all yours. Let's go have a look around."

Victoria accepted her father's arm. They'd obviously already seen the house, so it made sense to start outside. Showing off her newly damaged barn would mean disaster, so she steered him toward the bunk houses.

"Mr. Cartwright said you went to get some horses at an auction. Why didn't you call me? I could've called the breeder or at least gone with you to the auction."

"I did all right Daddy. Wait until you see the ones I brought back."

"You went alone?"

The shock in her father's voice was no surprise. Mr. Marana didn't think a woman should go anywhere alone. Why would they want to, when they could easily have a man with them?

She'd had a man with her, just not one she wanted to talk about with her father. She avoided mentioning Lang by saying, "I brought home four, the rest are being delivered."

"You talked the seller into delivering them for you? All the way out here? How'd you do that?"

Victoria turned away from her father's inquiring gaze.

He chuckled. "Never mind sweetie, you don't have to tell your father your tricks. I'm sure you used the Marana charm."

Was this the same man who gave every one of her dates the third degree? Why was it suddenly okay for her to charm some guy into doing anything, let alone come to her ranch? If she weren't so stressed out, Victoria would've asked him to explain himself.

When they arrived at the guest houses, her father pointed to the new door on Cactus Cabin. "I see you've got Hank is doing a fine job with the repairs."

Victoria sighed. "Hank and I have a deal. He takes care of the ranch stuff, like the barn and the tractor and I take care of the guest stuff, like these cabins."

Her father patted her shoulder. "Who took care of the door then?"

She groaned. Telling him the truth was probably going mean trouble but she wanted him to know she wasn't the unskilled idiot he accused her of being when she told him about her plans for The Circle Cat in the first place. "I hung the door."

In spite of her annoyance, Victoria took pleasure in seeing his jaw drop.

"I've watched you and your men do it dozens of times. Really, it's not that tricky."

Her father crossed his beefy arms across his thick chest and fixed her with a stern stare. "We talked about this before you left and you gave me your word that you wouldn't put yourself in danger."

"Hanging a door is not dangerous!" Victoria pulled her shoulders down and concentrated on sounding like a grown-up woman instead of an angry teenager. She appreciated his concern but she didn't like having to defend herself. "Really, I was careful."

Her dad shook his head, frowning. "You could've gotten hurt. It's not right for a little thing like you to do that kind of work. What if you'd gotten injured?"

"I'm fine. Besides, I'm not here alone."

"I know dear but Mr. Cartwright is an old man. What if you got in some real trouble? You need a strong, young, skilled hand here."

The image of Lang loading the horses popped into her mind. Strong. Young. He was all that—and more.

"If you're going to insist on doing these things, maybe I better talk to Susie about staying on for a few days. At least that way I can help you. And make sure everything is under control."

All the muscles Victoria had forced to relax tensed. She did not want her father taking over. There was only one way to stop him from staying. "Hank isn't the only one here."

"He's not?"

"There's another man." That much wasn't a lie. She hadn't said he worked for her.

Her father's eyebrows shot up. "Where is he? I want to meet him."

She gestured in the direction of the corral. "He's unloading the horses with Hank."

"Excellent. I'll get to check him out and see the horses at the same time."

Her father offered her his arm again. "Take me to them."

Victoria scrambled for of a way to get Lang aside before her father had a chance to interrogate him. All Lang had to do was nod when her father asked if he was working there. That way her dad and Susie would head back home and the whole crisis of having her father stick around would be solved.

"Don't you want to check on Susie?"

"No," he shook he head and took Victoria's arm. "I'm sure she's fine."

Her father started toward the smashed side of the barn, so she hurried after him to steer him around the way they'd come. One disaster at a time.

93

As Victoria led her father to the corral, Susie came skittering up waving her arms. She stumbled in her high heeled sandals but charged ahead across the small stones. With her carefully styled hair wind-blown and her eyes glowing against her flushed skin, it was obvious something was wrong. "Sammy! Something terrible's happened."

Mr. Marana dropped Victoria's arm, dashing over to his wife. "What is it honey? You okay?"

"I'm fine," she assured him with a girlish grin before her well-preserved face curved down. "It's my baby. I went out to move her out of that awful, dusty, driveway but she wouldn't start." Susie's green eyes filled with anguish.

Her father wrapped his arm around Susie and murmured something in her ear, then turned back to Victoria. "I'll be back as soon as I figure out what's wrong with the car."

Thankful for Susie's "baby" for the first time in her life, Victoria jogged around to the back of the trailer to find Lang.

He stood with one foot propped on the bottom fence rail and his tan arms folded across the top one. With the sun shining across his back he looked vital and alive.

Strong.

Capable.

Devastatingly sexy.

It was so right, seeing him standing there. As if he was a part of the ranch, as if he belonged at The Circle Cat.

An odd, unwelcome sense of disappointment settled through Victoria. Here she had an excellent chance to have everything she'd been working toward—and some carefree fun—and all she could do was stand around pining for what could never be.

What was wrong with her?

She needed to embrace that live-for-the-moment attitude.

How else was she going to have some carefree fun?

She'd made a deal with herself to live life on her own terms, to redefine herself and that was what she was determined to do.

So what if Lang made stupid assumptions about her. She'd prove him wrong. But first she had to get rid of her overprotective, bossy dad.

She called out to Lang and he turned. Time stalled as Victoria stared into his dark eyes, shivering in spite of the heat.

For a split second, an invitation lingered in his gaze, then it vanished and he shifted toward the animals. "They're settled."

Sasabe stamped her hooves in the far corner as she flicked her long, flaxen tail. The three other horses stood nearby, also eating from a small patch of grass, their coats glimmering in the sun.

There wasn't any reason for Lang to help her with the problem of her father but he was her only hope, so she had to work fast. She scurried over to him, glancing over her shoulder to be sure they were alone.

"Something on your mind, Victoria?"

Was she that obvious?

So what if she was, she didn't have any choice. "I have a favor to ask."

"Are we friends that you can ask me a favor?"

She'd gotten to know him well enough to recognize how the serious set of his mouth contrasted with his glimmering gaze when he was joking.

Using the same you-know-you-like-me expression she'd used on him the day before, she said, "Will you tell my father you're working here?"

The teasing flicker in his eyes evaporated. "I am working here, aren't I?"

She scanned his face, looking for a clue to tell her how to get what she wanted but ended up distracted by his dark afternoon stubble and glossy thick lashes. She pulled herself together by reminding herself her independence was at stake. "Yes, you're working here," she began cautiously, "If you could just not mention that it's temporary. Please."

He pushed his hat back, his expression unchanging. "Keeping secrets from daddy?"

Admitting that was unpleasant but appeared necessary. "He's worried about me being here by myself."

"You're not alone. Hank is here."

She wiggled closer, trying to distract him but seemed to only be distracting herself. "My dad is a little overprotective and he's worried that something might happen to me."

A crease appeared between Lang's eyebrows. "I seem to be missing something."

Victoria moved closer still and skimmed her fingertips across the collar of Lang's shirt. "My dad thinks I need a different kind of man around."

Lang's gaze flickered to her fingers, his voice dropping lower when he asked, "What kind of man does your dad think you need?"

Satisfaction warmed her when his throat jerked as he swallowed. She'd seen that reaction in him before and knew she'd brought it on. "To use his words," she trailed her fingers over the hard, tight plane of his chest, smiling inwardly when his muscles twitched. Following the buttons of his shirt, only stopping when her fingers hit the top of his silver belt buckle, she continued, "I need someone young… and strong." She tugged gently on the buckle, then added, "Skilled."

When she looked back up, the intensity of his desire-darkened gaze took her breath away and for a long second she lingered, her hand so near the rivets on his jeans that she could have had them undone in seconds.

He glanced over her shoulder, then back to her. "You trying to sweet-talk me, Miss Marana?"

She pulled in a shaky breath, the action made her stomach quiver and her center fill with heat. "Is it working?"

Lang covered Victoria's cheek with his palm. The silky smooth skin beneath his fingers warmed to his touch. She tucked her head into his hand, gazing up at him with eyes as clear as a cold morning.

For once her needs played right into his hand. Guilt sliced through him as she beamed at him with fresh innocence but he countered that inconvenient emotion with the notion that he'd been right all along. She was just like Lori Anne—using her feminine wiles to get what she wanted. Keeping his mind on that made not thinking about her unspoken promises a whole lot easier. Unspoken, not-going-to-happen promises. "I don't want to lie to your father."

"I don't want to lie to him either. Just tell him

you're working here," she pleaded, her fingers still holding onto his belt. "He'll assume it's permanent."

He lowered his hand, settled it at her waist, feeling the trim muscles of her waistline. If she knew what he was thinking, she'd be using that tender mouth to chew him out instead of tempting him with one of her sweet smiles. He almost grinned at the thought. He was pleasantly accustomed to her verbal jabs.

Her brow furrowed. "My dad said something about staying around, that's why I told him you were working here."

"Staying around?"

She looked away. "To keep an eye on me."

He hated the worry on her face. One long, uninterrupted kiss would scatter her troubles and he was the man to do it.

That and a lot more.

Lang roped in his racing libido and struggled for clear thoughts. Exposing her lie might get Victoria into trouble with Daddy Marana and be an easy way to get what he wanted.

No doubt the man had the power to force her to pack up and head home but getting dragged back to Phoenix kicking and screaming wouldn't be what was best for her in the long run. Forcing her hand wouldn't teach her the lesson she desperately needed to learn.

Lang couldn't stand the thought of her pretty head haunted by clouds of regret and disappointment. No, when she left the ranch, she'd go knowing that her future lay close to her family and friends. She'd be happy and content living where she belonged—back in Phoenix. With what Lang had in mind, that job was as good as done.

Chapter Nine

"Sorry about you havin' to put us up on such short notice, sweetheart. I checked Susie's car over before we left home but I suppose I wasn't as careful as I should've been." Victoria's father leaned back in the chair, wiping a few crumbs of toast off his cheek.

"No problem, dad. You had no way of knowing the starter was about to go bad. I'm just glad I had enough food for breakfast."

"When those chicks start laying, you won't have to worry about that." Susie stood up and took her husband's plate, stacking it on top of her own. "How soon will that be?"

After 60 long minutes of faking her way through answers to things like, "Where is the pump for the well?" and "Do you know how to shut the water off in case of an emergency?", Victoria was thankful for a question she knew the answer to. "About five months."

Susie piled the silverware over the plates. "After I saw Mr. Cartwright walk past the porch this morning, I followed him out to the barn. We changed the water, gave them some more feed. They're the cutest little things, all peeping and running around." She turned to her husband, "Have you been out to see them yet?"

Isabelle Drake

"Nope. I was too busy with the horses—what a beautiful herd. I'll take a look at the chicks when I go out to see how Lang's doing with the barn repairs."

Victoria stiffened to hold off the wild rush of longing that always accompanied her thoughts of Lang. "You don't have to worry about Lang, Daddy. He knows what he's doing."

"I've noticed that but since we're going to be here until that new starter gets delivered, I intend to make myself useful."

Susie reached across the table to pick up Victoria's plate. "That goes for me too. And I'm going to start by taking care of these dishes."

"That's sweet but you really don't need to, there's just—"

"Nonsense," Susie called over her shoulder as she hurried to the kitchen. "Your father and I love helping you." She peeked out through the doorway, "Whatever we can do for you, just way the word. Anything, anything at all. For the next few days, we're all yours."

That's what she was afraid of. Why couldn't they spend their time relaxing on the porch? Or playing cards? Victoria didn't even bother suggesting those alternatives. The two of them were bound and determined to help her whether she wanted them to or not.

So much for doing things on her own.

Her father pushed himself from the table and rolled to his feet. "You're coming with me, aren't you Victoria?"

If she let her father make himself useful on his own, there was no telling what he'd uncover. He'd probably find problems she hadn't even found herself.

"Of course she's coming with you." Susie zipped

back in, rounding the table to pick up the rest of the coffee cups, then pushing Victoria toward the door. "This ranch is her place."

Her father grumbled at Susie's comment but waited by the door, looking ready to take on a task even though his beefy arms were crossed over his chest.

Once they were outside, Victoria turned to her dad. "I know you don't want to waste time looking at those chicks. We can skip the barn too. Why don't we start by checking on the horses? It was dark last night when they were delivered. I had to use the flashlight, maybe—"

"Don't be silly," he took her arm and started toward the barn. "I know you want to look at those fluff balls. You always did have a soft spot for cute critters."

Like a lamb being led to slaughter, Victoria trailed beside her father. If only she didn't feel so inadequate and unprepared. If only she could shake the sense that her father was spending each minute looking for problems so he could bring them to her attention and point out her shortcomings.

That nagging worry, topped with her pent up, non-stop craving for Lang… it was all too much.

Beside the barn, Lang was bent over a makeshift pair of sawhorses. Despite the early hour, sweat glistened across his taut skin, making his shirt cling to his broad shoulders. Victoria tried to keep from gawking at the way his jeans pulled across his powerful thighs but she couldn't. Stepping closer was out of the question.

Even though he'd been giving her the cold

shoulder ever since he'd told her dad he was working at the ranch, she'd been thinking about him constantly. And seeing him was even worse. With him only a few feet away, all she could do was stare and ache with desire. Thinking about how alive she felt when he touched her, the way her body turned hot, liquid and expectant.

She held back, letting her father move away from her side, closer to Lang.

"Morning, Lang," her father called as he marched forward to inspect the boards piled near a box of nails. "We missed you at breakfast. You aren't on one of those crazy liquid diets are you?"

"No, sir."

"Glad to hear it. Susie was real disappointed when you didn't come to dinner last night. She claims she's never met a real cowboy before. She says all the ones she's met just had a bad case of cow fever."

Lang chuckled but didn't look up from the boards he was measuring. He ran the tape across the wood, his biceps popping out of his rolled up shirtsleeves.

"We'll see you at lunch?" her dad pressed. "I don't want Susie disappointed two days in a row."

Lang stood, wiping the back of his hand across his tanned forehead. He turned and his gaze flashed past Victoria to settle somewhere in the pasture. "I'll be there for lunch."

"That's settled then." Her father continued on toward the barn, his sturdy legs moving quickly across the dust and dirt. "Come on, sweetheart, let's go look at your birds."

Victoria's gaze zigzagged from her father's swaying back to the pile of boards, then on its own, focused on Lang's rugged face. "Thanks for working on the barn."

He barely glanced at her as he reached for the saw and lined it up with the pencil marks he'd made. "I said I'd do it."

"Still," she paused, trying to think of something to say. "I appreciate it. Um, thanks."

"No problem," he muttered, uninterested.

Although almost everything about Lang confused Victoria, one thing she knew for certain was that he had a firm sense of right and wrong. He probably resented being made part of the deceit with her father.

There wasn't anything more to say, so she sidestepped in the direction her father had gone.

"Victoria?"

She turned to find Lang staring at her, his mouth set, his velvety eyes searching.

"I know you wanted to do all this by yourself but your father and Susie, really care about you. They're your family—and family is what matters. Not ranches. Or success. You're lucky to have them. Don't forget that."

Without waiting for her to respond, he turned back around, sliding the handsaw back and forth with sharp, jerky motions.

Obviously he was relating to her situation somehow.

How?

His ex-wife?

She must've hurt him badly. With a pang of jealousy, Victoria assumed he must've loved her deeply. A woman would have to be a total fool to walk away from a man like Lang.

What kind of woman was Lori Anne?

Funny? Smart? Pretty?

Had she enjoyed taking care of Lang?

Those questions would never have answers. Right after she slipped into the barn, Hank jogged through the door at the opposite end. His words tumbled out between breaths, "Miss Marana, the horses… did you… move them?"

She stepped back, trying to make sense of Hank's question.

"The horses… your new herd… did you move them?"

Alarm gripped Victoria, flashing through her body and making her muscles tense. "Move them?"

Her father strode across the dirt floor, his stout arms swinging at his sides. "What's the problem? What's going on?"

Hank's gaze darted between them, then he ran his hands over his flushed face. "The horses aren't in the corral. They're not there, they're gone."

Icy fear slashed through Victoria. "Gone?"

"The gate's wide open and the corral is empty."

Empty?

It didn't make sense.

"I thought you did a head count last night," Hank said. "Miss Marana, did you double check that latch?"

Victoria crammed her fingers through her hair. "Of course I did." But she'd been so tired, after everything that had happened with Lang, then her father and Susie showing up…

Maybe she hadn't been careful enough.

She raced past Hank and her father, through the door and on to the corral. The area was empty. Her beautiful animals were nowhere in sight.

How could she have let this happen?

"What should I do Miss Marana?" Hank asked as he reached the open gate. Her father was close behind. The two men stared at her, waiting for her to do something, say something.

Worry for the animals' safety and well-being chased away her embarrassment. "Can you ride bareback, Hank?"

"Of course but—"

"We'll each take a bucket of feed, a lead rope and a bridle. Use the feed to lure the first horse you find, then mount up. These animals know each other, so once we find one, we'll probably find the rest. Bring the ones you find to the corral, then go back out.

"I'll go get the feed buckets, Hank you get the leads, dad you get bridles." Victoria started for the small shed where they kept the feed. "We'll meet back here, then split up."

* * *

The sun hung directly overhead when Victoria led the last horse into the corral. Sweat ran into her eyes and down her back. Fatigue clung to her like a second skin.

She accepted the jug of water her father offered as soon as she latched the gate and took a long drink. "I still don't understand how it came open," she said.

"It's done and over with now. Come on up to the house. Susie made lunch."

Victoria took another drink from the jug then nodded weakly. "She didn't want to miss out on meeting a real cowboy?"

Her dad laughed as he wrapped his thick arm around her weary shoulders. "That—and it gave her something to do while she worried about me falling off. It's been a while since I've ridden bareback."

"You could've taken a saddle with you."

"No, you were right. If we tried to lug saddles we wouldn't have been able to move as fast." He brushed his hand across her back. "You impressed me, honey. I didn't realize you could think so fast."

Did her father's compliment mean he was finally accepting her choice? Victoria was too bushed to decide. "Thanks."

Inside, Lang and Susie were seated at the table, laughing like old friends. He turned and grinned at Victoria, his gaze skimming across her weary muscles. "You look as tired as a mule that walked a mile in East Texas mud."

Victoria scowled, ignoring the constant vibrations that hummed through her whenever he was around. "I'm not impressed with your cowboy charm."

He laughed as she dropped into her seat with a groan of disgust, then said, "You could've told me you needed help."

She didn't have the energy to deal with the rush of emotions he let lose, so she did her best to ignore him, turning instead to her stepmother. "Thanks for making lunch, Susie," she said, gesturing to the stacks of sandwiches and bowls of sliced fruit.

The other woman beamed. "It was no trouble." Then looking out into the yard, she asked, "Where's Hank?"

"He's worn out, so he'll be up after a while."

"I'll join you all after I get the pie out of the oven, you all go ahead and get started."

Victoria didn't have to be asked twice. She piled her plate with food and dug in.

Lang scooped some fruit out of the bowl. "Your paneling was delivered while you were out chasing the horses."

The mouthful of salami and cheese kept her from replying but her father chuckled. "I had to chase down a few but from what I can tell, my little girl just sweet talked them in."

Lang turned a skeptical gaze her way. "That so?" Was it her imagination or did he seem bugged by her father's praise?

She shrugged and picked up the fruit bowl while her father continued. "If I didn't know better, I'd think Victoria had been taking riding lessons from a rodeo pro instead of that stiff lipped coach at the stable."

Although the compliment was indirect, a warm sense of satisfaction and acceptance flowed through Victoria. Maybe her dad was starting to see that she was capable. Maybe he'd see things her way by the time that starter arrived. She could only hope, then he'd finally butt out of her life.

Susie sashayed into the room, humming and smiling. "That pie is for after dinner, so don't ask for any before then." After she put half a sandwich on her plate she swiveled, giving Lang her full attention. "Now you can finish that wonderful story."

Victoria only half listened to Lang's irritating yarn about the time his cousin dared him to ride blindfolded through town and his horse stepped on the sheriff's hat.

Oh please.

Blindfolded.

Hmmm... now if he were blindfolded for her pleasure, that wouldn't be so bad.

107

In fact, the more she thought about it the more she warmed up to the idea. There might be something wickedly sinful about having her way with a man who couldn't see her, he wouldn't know what to expect.

She'd start by popping those buttons, like she'd thought about that first day in the bunkhouse.

No, back up.

First she'd tie him to one of those rough posts near the fat, pot belly stove, binding his wrists gently behind his back with soft twine. That way she could do whatever she wanted. He wouldn't be able to walk away just when things were going the way she wanted.

After she pulled his shirt open, she'd spread her fingers across the hard muscles of his chest, trail her fingertips over the tight curves of his stomach. Then she'd loosen that belt he always wore, unzip his jeans, ready to get an answer to what she'd been wondering—did that bulge look as big outside his pants as it did in?—slide her hand and—"

"Victoria? Honey? You okay dear?"

Victoria blinked. "Wh-what?"

Susie shook her head, a knowing smile lighting up her face. "Never you mind dear, I'm sure your face is just flushed from all that sun, that's all."

Good grief.

Victoria slumped in her chair, managing, just barely, to not roll her eyes at her own stupidity.

* * *

"Bath time ladies."

Cassie, Prickly Pear and Sasabe eyed Victoria warily as she tugged at the hose. "Don't look at me like that. You want to be pretty for our guests tomorrow don't you?"

Not willing to be put off by their lack of enthusiasm, Victoria tossed down the bottle of horse shampoo, then jogged back to the yard hydrant. When she got back, Hank was scratching Cassie's neck.

As always, he tipped his hat. "Afternoon, Miss Marana," he said over Cassie's nickers.

Victoria nodded to the black pony. "She's a sweet little one."

"That she is. You gettin' these girls cleaned up for the opening tomorrow?"

"Yep. I don't know how they got so dirty but I want everything perfect for our first day with guests."

As she ran the hose across the pony's back, she turned to Hank. "I finished the paneling in Cactus Cabin and the trim in Paradise Hideaway this morning. Susie and dad are hanging the curtains and putting on the fresh sheets right now." A grin split across her face. "We're actually ready on time."

"That's wonderful, Miss Marana." The old hand stepped back to keep from getting sprayed. "I got the feelin' you weren't so happy about your dad being here but he and Miss Susie sure have pitched in."

Victoria chuckled. "You're right on both counts, Hank."

"Miss Susie says they'll be on their way either tonight or first thing tomorrow."

Scooting around to douse the pony's tail, she asked hopefully, "The delivery man brought the new starter?"

"Not yet, he called to say he'd be out here later today."

Hank stepped onto the path that led to the bunkhouse. "I'm going to rest a spell."

"That's a great idea." She waved him on. "I'll send Lang down to get you when dinner's ready."

The old man took a few steps, then paused. "You've got a lot to be proud of."

Affection washed over her. Hank had done so much for her, she never would've been ready without his help. Words of thanks stuck in her throat, so she nodded.

Hank turned, waving over his shoulder. Victoria moved from Cassie to hose down Sasabe. The horse nudged her elbow then swung its head around to watch the bright wildflowers tip in the slight breeze.

When she'd left home, Victoria never would've thought she'd be grateful for help from her father and Susie. Just the idea of Susie helping had been foreign. But she had and without complaining.

For the second, or maybe it was the third time, Victoria realized she'd never really given her stepmother a chance. She'd always assumed the perfectly dressed, carefully preserved woman she saw every day was all there was to Susie. She'd been wrong about that.

"Okay, Prickly Pear, it's your turn." Victoria held the hose low, ran water across the mare's front left hoof and then slowly raised the stream of water. "So far, so good. Now let's do your back."

The animal only flicked its tail once, then stood quietly while Victoria continued to wet her down. "That's a good girl, we'll be done in no time, then I can put my feet up for a few minutes before cooking dinner." Soon the Appaloosa's coat was sleek with moisture.

Pleasure settled around Victoria. She was proud of what she'd achieved but like Hank suggested, she knew that without the help of her family she never would've been ready on time. She'd been wrong about having to do everything on her own too. It was okay to take help from some people, like family. It didn't lessen her accomplishment.

Once Prickly Pear was completely wet, Victoria reached for the shampoo bottle and twisted off the cap. The gentle wind caught the strange scent of the thick, yellow liquid and she frowned at the mares.

"Smells a little yucky," she held up the bottle, "But see how pretty she looks on the label? You girls will look twice that good. Even you, Prickly Pear."

Washing all three at once would be a great way to save time so she poured four, fat puddles on each horse's back.

"Victoria?"

Susie rounded the corner of the barn and tottered over. "Have you seen the cooking oil? I was sure you had a big bottle of it in the cupboard and I've looked everywhere for it but it's just not there. I'm making Lang a surprise for dinner and I can't make it without that oil."

Victoria stretched up on her toes to rub the slippery shampoo across Cassie's dark coat. "I can make dinner tonight, Susie."

"I know but, well, Lang's been talking about how much he loves authentic Mexican food and I want to make him some homemade tortilla chips to go with that salsa I made yesterday."

"You're spoiling him, Susie." Bubbly, white foam rose up, mounding across the horse's back.

111

"Don't worry, I explained to him that once I'm gone he won't be getting any more special treatment and that—"

"Afternoon ladies."

"Lang." Susie picked her way across the streams of sudsy water rippling across the ground. "Have you been eavesdropping on us?"

"Course not. I just happened by."

Victoria turned her gaze away from his wicked grin and concentrated on sweeping her arms down Cassie's chest, the foam continuing to build. It got so thick it dripped onto the ground, making little white mountains on the dark brown dirt.

"Getting those mares good and clean, Victoria?"

Instead of answering, she left the pony, moving to start rubbing the shampoo across Sasabe. What could he want? Ever since her father and Susie had arrived, he'd all but ignored her. She'd been painfully aware of him yet the days passed easily enough for him.

While her arms stretched across the mare's golden back, her gaze locked with Lang's. Irritation flickered through her.

Why was he staring at her like that? Despite the sun's bright rays, a shiver wiggled down her arms and she found herself unable to look away, the answer to her question forming in her mind.

"Answer me Lang Thompson!"

Lang finally got momentary control of himself and jerked his head away from Victoria. "Sorry, Susie... I... Do you need me to do something?"

Susie planted her fists on her slim hips. "I asked you three times if you'd seen the cooking oil. I can't make tortilla chips without it."

"Tortilla chips?"

"That's right. Homemade tortilla chips. But there won't be any without that cooking oil."

Lang glanced at the mounds of heavy foam growing on Sasabe's neck. Victoria's tanned arms continued to sway in enticing, rhythmic circles as she lathered the horse's mane.

Hours of watching her from a distance and the rest of the time thinking about her and that kiss she'd laid on him—he was steaming hard, like a tea kettle that couldn't whistle.

After pulling in a long, steadying breath, he tore his gaze away. "You look in the cupboard?" he asked, even though he knew for a fact it wasn't there.

"Of course." Susie threw her hands at him. "Never mind. I don't know why I asked you in the first place."

Why hadn't he put that oil back right away? He chanced another glance at Victoria's long legs but instead of turning away quickly, he took his time admiring the way her bare skin was covered with shimmering droplets of glistening water and her sweet, round ass wiggled each time she moved.

The back of her pink t-shirt clung to her shoulders, hinting at the dip of her waist. The front of her shirt had to be soaked. Her nipples would probably be hard, tight and begging for heat. His mouth watered and his blood headed south, swelling his cock.

Lordy, if she turns around…

"I'll make something else. Eggs?" Susie's foot crunched lightly on the gravel as she stepped away. "We can have scrambled eggs and salsa."

Eggs?

113

No homemade chips?

"Wait, Susie, maybe, it's... it's up high where you can't see it. Wait here and I'll go look on the top shelf, okay? I'll bet it's up there."

She curved one of her perfectly shaped eyebrows at him and smirked. "Don't you think I thought of that? I used a chair to check."

"I'll go find it." He waved at her, insisting that she wait, as he jogged toward the house—and away from Victoria.

Chapter Ten

"Looks like Lang is almost done," Susie said.

Victoria glanced at the barn. Newly hung siding covered the space that had been the gaping hole. He'd have it stained by tomorrow afternoon and then the only reminder of Lang's presence would be his horses.

Her horses, she corrected.

Susie's curious gaze bore into Victoria, so to avoid the questions that always seemed to follow her stepmother's scrutiny, she turned to Prickly Pear. "Okay crabby girl, your turn." She ran her palms across the horse's back and circled her hands through the puddles of shampoo. The slick foam expanded with each swipe and soon the mare's back was glistening, glimmering under the sun.

"You're lucky to have someone like Lang around."

Victoria definitely did not want to talk about Lang so she took the opportunity to tell Susie something she'd been wanting to find the right time to say. "You know Susie, you and Dad have been great. I really appreciate everything you've done."

Susie tipped her head, noticing the change in conversation no doubt. "We're family, you don't need to thank me."

"Yes. I do." Victoria shoved the pile of foam across Prickly Pear's haunches. "After I made such a big deal about doing everything by myself, you and Dad could've sat back and watched me fail."

Susie tiptoed around the streaming rivulets and growing piles of foam, her pink sandals catching the sun's rays. "You wouldn't have failed."

"I wouldn't have been ready on time. Like I am now." Knowing that she'd never really made the effort to connect with her stepmother, she added, "Really, thanks for everything."

Susie nodded, accepting the gratitude with her typical grace and pointed a long flashy, pink nail at Prickly Pear. "Is that shampoo supposed to foam up like that?"

It did seem strange, the way the foam grew with every swing of her hand. But then she'd never used horse shampoo before. "It ought to get them good and clean."

"I guess so, if you ever get it rinsed off."

Victoria hadn't thought of that. The fat layer of lather coating Prickly Pear's back didn't look like it would ever rinse off. Clumps of bubbles clung to Sasabe's glossy mane and Cassie's thick legs were sleek and well-coated with the glossy residue of the shampoo.

"The cooking oil is on the counter." Lang huffed over to stand squarely in front of Susie. "So there's no problem. We can have the chips, right?"

Susie patted her hair, studying him as she pressed her smoothly glossed lips together. "If I didn't know better, I'd think you hid it just to make me crazy."

Lang's eyebrows twisted. "Hide it? Why would... What-what would I want with cooking oil?"

Susie laughed as she hopped across the quickly expanding bubble rimmed puddles. "I didn't really mean it. From what I've seen, I'm not sure you have enough gumption to do anything like that."

He frowned. "What's that supposed to mean?"

"Never mind." Susie said over her shoulder, tiptoeing around the puddles as she started for the house. "See you both at dinner."

"What do you think she meant by that?" Lang asked Victoria once Susie was out of earshot. "I've got gumption." He spread his arms wide. "Don't you think?"

Victoria peeked under Prickly Pear's mane to take a long look at Lang's delicious broad chest and rock-hard forearms. "I guess so," she replied, not thinking about gumption at all. Then, realizing she sounded ungrateful for the work he'd done, added, "You did fix the barn. It looks good. Perfect. Thanks."

After a pause, he replied, "It'll be done as soon as I stain it."

And then he'd be gone.

She glanced from Lang to the barn then nodded but didn't say anything. What was there to add?

She was living the life she'd wanted. She should be happy and fulfilled. Proud of her accomplishments. Anxious to take what she wanted from the world. So Lang wasn't her Mr. Right For a Night. She'd find another. There had to be plenty of men who'd like to have some spur-of-the-moment fun.

Still, each time she told herself her dream was coming true, that she had everything she'd wished for, she found herself thinking that her life wasn't complete. A hefty gaping hole lingered in her world and it seemed to be getting wider each day.

Lang moved closer and looked at the horses. "Are they clean enough yet?"

Her conflicted thoughts evaporated when she scanned the animals. Even Prickly Pear looked sweet and approachable. Slick bubbles ran down her side and plopped onto the ground.

Victoria caught Lang watching her, his gaze taking in the wet cling of her clothes, the way her t-shirt was plastered to each breast, outlining each tight nipple. She shifted under his stare and he didn't miss a single, tiny movement.

That awesome sense of power, the one she'd felt when she kissed him behind the horse trailer, came back with a vengeance. "Don't you have something better to do than stand around and harass me?" she asked, angling her hips toward him and bending lower than necessary as she reached for the hose with deliberate slowness.

To her satisfaction, he climbed onto the fence rail and tucked his hands into his back pockets, as though he didn't trust himself to keep his hands to himself. The breeze pressed his blue plaid shirt against his flat stomach, making the delicious curve below his belt even more noticeable. He was quiet for several long minutes, then finally asked, "Think you'll be done by dinner? Or should I tell Susie to give me your food?"

"You and those stupid homemade tortilla chips," she replied, smiling as she twisted to spray Cassie's front legs.

Instead of rinsing clean, the shampoo fought back by generating more bubbles. The harder she sprayed, the more lather appeared. How was that possible?

The weight of Lang's curious stare continued to

weigh on her back, so she left Cassie to spray down Sasabe. Again the shampoo fought back, raising more bubbles instead of rinsing clean. That simmering sexual tension fizzled into frustration and a reluctant bit of embarrassment.

The minutes dragged. Even after spraying Sasabe down from haunch to hoof, the mare was still coated with slick lather. By the time Victoria moved on to Prickly Pear, not only did she look as though she'd been thoroughly hosed down herself but she was as crabby as the spotted mare who earned her name by being stubborn and unwilling.

"You need some help, Victoria?"

Why couldn't he have been there when she rounded up the horses, instead of catching her mess up something as simple as washing the mares? She cast him a scowl. "Not from you, thank you very much."

He lifted his eyebrows, amusement circling his face. When Victoria followed his gaze with her own, she spotted Cassie about to give Sasabe a nip on the rump. Prickly Pear had her ears pinned down and was flicking her tail. At the rate she was going, there was no way the horses were going to wait patiently for dinner while she finished rinsing them off.

She couldn't take them to the corral in their sticky state but she could bring part of their dinner to them. "Wait here, girls. I'll get some hay."

After getting three feedbags, she crossed to the barn where a newly delivered stack of hay bales waited to be moved to the small shed used to store feed. With the bags flapping against her side, she marched to the stacks and reached for a low bale on the end.

119

Isabelle Drake

Once Victoria disappeared, Lang hopped down and followed her into the barn. That cooking oil added to the shampoo did the trick every time. Even though she hadn't said anything about the never-ending lather, she'd gotten plenty frustrated.

All she needed now was a little something more—a gentle shove—and she'd be ready to cry uncle. A few careless words blurted out in front of daddy Marana and she'd be rethinking the whole I-want-to-run-a-dude-ranch thing and the ranch would be back on the market.

Problem solved—his and hers.

Lang tried to avoid gazing at the way her long, tan legs flexed as she moved but the pull was too fierce.

He wouldn't get sidetracked by her sexy body—or that horse bath scene. He couldn't have daydreamed up a hotter scenario. If he ever went into the business of making porn, he knew where to start.

Don't think about that hose.

Or her wet shirt. Slick with shampoo and clinging to her smooth, soft skin.

He held his breath, tense with anticipation as she wrapped her fingers around the twine he'd snipped about an hour ago then winced when her shoulders jerked back, jutting her rib cage forward. Lang swallowed against the lump that formed in his suddenly dry throat.

Just as he expected the twine whirled free, scattering clumps of hay across the floor of the barn. Victoria stumbled but instead of falling back, she fought to right herself and ended up tumbling across the bale, falling face first into the lose hay.

120

Pieces stuck to her damp arms, got tangled in her hair. The more she struggled, the more the hay clung to her. When she spotted him, her gaze narrowed and she immediately stopped scrambling.

The heated flush of simmering frustration brightened her cheeks and darkened her eyes. Lang's gaze traced the outline of her round breasts as her chest rose and fell with each sharp breath, then shifted to her firm legs, draped across one of the bales.

Struggling to right herself by pushing up with one hand, she cast him a warning glance, "You want something?"

Hell yes, he wanted something.

Penned-in need, hours of very detailed fantasizing and pure old-fashioned lust finally got the better of him and he let go of the promise he'd made to keep his emotions fenced in and safe from harm.

Not thinking with his cock? He'd never *really* considered that. Had he?

He covered the distance between them in three strides. After swinging over the hay bales, he pushed her back until she was nestled in the hay and swiftly covered her mouth with his own.

She welcomed him eagerly, softening her lips and angling her head back to give herself over to him. Her sigh whispered across his lips, in response he swept his tongue across hers and deepened the kiss.

The softness of her skin, that tantalizing citrus scent that followed her everywhere and the over-the-top need to have her, made his movements fevered and fast.

His hands couldn't move quickly enough, her skin was damp and cool but turned warm everywhere he put his hands. "I need to touch what I've been staring at and dreaming about."

"What are you waiting for?"

He tugged up her damp shirt then cupped her round breasts, lifting the soft mounds higher, freeing them from her simple white bra. She arched her back, pushing her sweet flesh into his hands as he lightly flicked the tips with his thumbs. She pulled in a sharp breath, instinctively spreading her legs to bring him closer. But it wasn't nearly enough—he wanted to touch her everywhere at once—inside and out.

She shifted beneath him, moving so his rigid cock pressed firmly against her soft center. He responded by reaching around to grab her ass with both of his hands and press against her, wishing like hell their clothes were already off.

Sill matching his demanding kisses, she slid her hands up under his shirt and skimmed her palms across his back, the heat from her hands seeping through his skin, tormenting him, making him even more desperate for real contact, the all-over skin-to-skin kind.

Pressing harder into her, he slipped his hands up to the small of her back, she moaned, arching up to give him easier access. The velvety skin beneath his fingers was even more incredible than he'd imagined. The gentle glide of her tongue across his—mind-blowing.

How could she be so sweet and unskilled at seduction, yet so demanding and sexy at the same time?

It was as though the heavens had taken everything he'd wanted in a woman and given it to Victoria.

When he lowered his mouth to graze along her jaw she whispered something that made his roaming hands halt. "I thought you said I wasn't *this* kind of woman."

Dazed, he lifted his head and gazed into her passion-drunk eyes that were sparking with something he didn't understand, then she said another thing he didn't want to hear. It wasn't so much the words, as her tone. Female satisfaction edged with I-told-you-so.

"Change your mind about me, cowboy?"

She ran her tongue across her lips, her gaze fixed on his mouth as she arched a brow and asked, "Nothing to say? Not ready to admit you were wrong?"

What could he say? That he'd changed his mind, he thought she was the type of woman worth fooling around with but not worth staying around for?

He couldn't say that, it was a lie. The complete opposite of the truth.

Resolutely, she straightened her clothes then wiggled free and scrambled to her feet. Grabbing handfuls of hay to stuff into the feedbags, she said, "Well, Lang. I haven't changed my mind about you."

She marched through the barn, leaving a trail of hay behind her, and ducked out of the barn without even a parting glance.

She hadn't changed her mind about him? What the hell did she mean by that?

Lang sagged back, groaning as he ran his hand over his throbbing hard-on, a very reluctant smile pulling across his well-kissed mouth. She made him feel alive, strong, capable. But she also made him confused. But even worse than that, desperate with need.

Hot, impulsive actions were fine, when no feelings were involved. But the constant hunger he felt

123

for Victoria—it scared him. Bad. He'd trusted once and lost everything that meant anything to him.

Staring out to the sunshine, he imagined Victoria back out with the mares. In that wet t-shirt. Bending, her slick skin glimmering in the sun.

Damn. He had to stop. Thinking about her that way was nothing but trouble.

He tried to convince himself they were both better off, that he was glad she'd walked out on him.

But it didn't work. He was too far gone and he knew it.

* * *

The homemade chips and fresh salsa sat on the table when Lang crossed into the dining room. Victoria's father and Susie huddled together, whispering and enjoying each other the way they often did.

When Sam spotted him in the doorway, the other man tilted back and laid his arm behind his wife. "Victoria will be right out. Washing up those horses was a big job."

Lang nodded, settling into the chair opposite Sam. He'd taken to sitting there because it kept Victoria, who sat at the head of the table, out of his direct line of sight. But he'd had as much success not watching her every move as he had at not thinking about her all the time. In a word, none.

Now, after that kiss, with fresh impressions of her exploring hands, her needy welcoming touch…

He held in a groan.

Susie smoothed a hair into place. "You look worn out, Lang."

He bobbed his head up and down. That was the ticket. He needed rest—alone—and far away from curvaceous, female enticement. "Hank's so tired he's skipping dinner."

"Hank's not eating? Is he okay?" Victoria swept into the room, holding the same pitcher she'd used that first day on the porch.

"He's fine, just wiped out." Lang was grateful Victoria had changed out of her wet clothes but he didn't need a picture to remember how she'd looked. That explosive image—and what happened in the barn—would be with him forever.

If he hadn't lost control, if he'd kept his mind on the business of getting Victoria to see she didn't belong at the ranch, instead of jumping on her like the hormone-crazed man he was, everything would've been fine. As fine as things can be when a man is going out of his way to avoid a woman he's thinking about every minute of the day and dreaming about every minute he's in bed.

Susie flashed a bright smile Victoria's way. "You look a bit tired yourself, sweetie."

Victoria's gaze skipped around the room, going everywhere but on him. "Running this place is hard work but you don't hear me complaining." She slumped into her chair with a sigh. "I'm sorry Susie. I guess I'm on edge. With the guests coming tomorrow and everything… There's a lot going on."

And she'd been handling it as though she'd been managing life at The Circle Cat for years instead of weeks. There was the problem. Every time Lang tried to prove Victoria didn't belong at the ranch, she'd managed to show off some secret skill or obscure hidden talent.

125

Roping down those horses he let loose, for one example. Another—the way she unknowingly turned the tables on him with that X-rated, wet t-shirt horse bath. How was he supposed to see something like that coming? Or that episode in the hay stacks? The frustration factor alone would drive any sane man as crazy as a lizard with sunstroke.

With the barn almost done, he was just about out of time. No wonder tension tugged at his every nerve, Lang mused. Saving a woman from herself had never been so difficult. Not that he'd tried to do it before. Still, how was he supposed to know it was going to be so infuriating?

Susie and Mr. Marana exchanged a scheming glance, the gleam in their eyes making his skin prickle. Lang eyed the chips, put his napkin in his lap and asked stiffly, "Everyone ready to eat?"

So Lang was hungry?

Victoria ignored his question and made a point of very, very carefully carving off a serving of roast as slowly as she could without remaining still, laying it on her plate in the most leisurely way possible and then passing the platter to her father. Out of the corner of her eye, she watched her dad serve Susie, himself and then pass the roast onto Lang whose face was pulled so tight he looked like he was ready to burst.

Served him right. At least she'd gotten the better of him—again.

Her father pointed at the big bowl in front of her. "Will you start the chips?"

She forced a bright smile, heaped the biggest, tastiest looking chips onto her plate and then passed the bowl—in the opposite direction from Lang. If he ended up with crumbs, well, that wouldn't be her fault, would it?

"I've enjoyed cooking a few of our meals but your food is better, Victoria." Susie said, pointing to the odd mixture of roast, chips with salsa and some mysterious vegetable dish. "Yours is more ranch-like."

"Thanks, Susie," she responded warmly. Connecting with her stepmother was an unexpected benefit of having her parents stranded at the ranch.

"Susie's right, honey. You've done an excellent job with everything." Her dad raised his fork, gestured to Lang, "Don't you think so?"

"Yes, sir." Lang's reply was so stiff she was surprised the words didn't drop out of the air like chunks of frozen rain.

Victoria shot a look his way, the usual chilly cloud she expected to see in his eyes wasn't there. Instead, his gaze was intense and searching. A river of heat rushed through her veins.

A hot and cold cowboy.

Who knew such a thing existed?

"Those horses are coming along well, honey."

"I think so too," she moved her gaze to her stepmother. "Susie and I had a great ride this morning."

"We sure did." Susie patted her husband's arm, "You missed out, sweetie pie." She turned a wily expression to Lang. "You go out with Victoria yet, Lang?"

Victoria peered at Lang from the corner of her eye and for a split second she thought she saw a touch of something volatile in his dark gaze. Regret? For letting her walk away in the barn? Or was she imagining that because that's what she wanted to see?

Lang's gaze shifted to Susie. "No, ma'am. We haven't been out yet."

Susie appeared to be oblivious to the tension vibrating across the table, as she tisk-tisked his non-committal reply. "You two better go first thing tomorrow morning."

Victoria nearly choked on her chips. Survive time alone with him? Sure, she could get him to kiss her. What then… and would whatever came next, be enough?

After a few hard swallows and a long drink of iced tea, she managed to speak up. "Tomorrow morning?"

"Yes, of course. While your dad is finishing with the starter. You two go on out and take one last ride to check the trails. Make sure the horses are ready for the guests."

Lang's gaze bounced between Victoria and Susie. "We'll have plenty of time on the trails, um… next week."

"Oh, Lang," Susie's manicured nails danced in the air, "You won't get in a good, hard ride with those tenderfoots along."

"I think Susie's right," her dad broke in. "You need to go out, just the two of you. You've been so busy with the other horses, Sasabe hasn't gone out in days."

Victoria turned to Lang for help but he shrugged in defeat. "Guess we could head out tomorrow… sometime… "

"Right after breakfast." Susie's chin dipped down, settling the matter.

Chapter Eleven

Lang rubbed his eyes and moaned.

"Morning! Too tired to sleep, cowboy?" Hank's chuckle rattled around the bunkhouse.

Lang managed to open one eye. A bright shaft of southwestern sun pierced his pupil, making him snap his eyelid shut.

"You were tossin' and turnin' all night, son. Something on your mind?"

Yeah, Susie's not so innocent words "good hard ride".

That woman knew exactly what she was saying and how he'd react to it. She probably had a history of stirring up trouble.

"Something on your mind?" Hank repeated.

Obviously the old man had his strength back. At least one of them had slept well. "No, Hank. Nothing's on my mind."

"Could've fooled me."

Lang cast him a warning glance. "Don't you have some busted piece of equipment to fix?"

"Nope." The old man grinned, shoving his hands into his coveralls and propping himself against one of the wood beams. "Thanks to Sam and Susie, I've had more than enough time to get everything up and running."

"Good for you," Lang grumbled, rolling himself upright, still struggling to get his eyes open.

Hank chortled at Lang's distress. "I'm planning on taken' it easy this morning, check things over one last time. Make sure everything is safe and secure." The old hand swung away from the post, continuing without giving Lang to reply. "You still planning on leaving today?"

"Yep." He didn't have any choice. He was out of time and out of luck.

"When you hittin' the road?" the man asked, reaching down to straighten the cover on his bed.

"Victoria and I are going for a ride this morning. Then, after Sam and Susie go, I'll pack up."

Hank titled his head, glanced over at Lang. "A trail ride? Just you and Miss Marana?"

"Yeah, it was Susie's idea."

The old man gave the cover one last tug then straightened, his mouth pulling to the side. "I see."

"Sasabe hasn't gone out with the others. She's the only one that hasn't been out on the trails, so we need to take her out." The explanation sounded lame even to Lang but it was the only one he had.

The hand tucked his chin in, peering down at him. "I see."

"Then, after Sam and Susie leave, I'll come in and pack."

Hank stayed put, staring down at him. "So you said."

Lang sighed as he swung his legs over the edge of the bed, carefully avoiding the other man's gaze. "Tell Victoria I'll be up for breakfast in a few minutes."

"Okay," he replied but lingered a moment longer.

About the time Lang thought he was going to say something more, the old man spun himself around and ambled out.

Lang gritted his teeth and threw the covers aside. His back was stiff and his eyelids felt like sandpaper. So much for getting one, final, good night of sleep. Holding in a curse of complaint, he pushed himself up and hobbled to the shower.

Once the water rolled down his back, he leaned on the tiled wall, trying to sort the thoughts and images that had kept him awake most of the night. It all boiled down to one word.

Victoria.

The temptation to touch her each time he saw her, the longing to step close enough to smell her hair, the desire to taste her lips and the all-consuming need to make love to her thrummed constantly across each nerve ending.

Lang glanced down at his quickly rising cock and hit the hot water fixture, spinning it around until it stopped. Cold, he definitely needed cold.

The repair on the barn was complete. Sam and Susie would soon be on their way. There was nothing holding him back, nothing keeping him from leaving The Circle Cat. His time was up.

He'd never know if Victoria was sweet and tender when she gave herself to a man or if she was bold and demanding. More likely, she was an untamed mixture of give and take, easy but wanton. Days with a woman like her would never be dull and the nights…

Lang reached down to stroke his solid shaft.

Damn.

She'd gotten to him again.

131

His grip tightened with frustration and need, his movements turning sharp and quick. He didn't even bother holding back his groans. Denying his feelings would be as pointless as his efforts to shake sense into Victoria. How she'd managed to turn each one of his schemes into an opportunity to succeed at the impossible he'd never know. He rejected the obvious, that she had what it took be a rancher and she belonged at The Circle Cat.

Instead, he focused on what he wanted to be the truth. That Victoria was a spoiled rich girl playing at running a business. That was his last defense against the impossible—falling in love with Victoria Marana.

His cock jerked with release, Lang sagged against the cold tiles. He had to face facts.

She'd be staying on, he'd be headed south. Had he let himself down? Or was it Victoria who'd eventually pay the price for his failure to get her to face the truth? What would happen after he left?

Disaster. That's what.

She'd discover that she belonged in Phoenix but she'd learn the hard way. A failure wouldn't break her forever, she was too determined for that. Still, it would give her spirit a beating—slow her down and keep her from the life he believed she wanted. A husband and children.

That business about being a good time girl—that could lead to more trouble than she could ever imagine.

Like a dog with a bone, he clamped onto the slim possibility of finding a way to get Victoria to see that she didn't really belong there. All he needed was one more chance. He'd watch for the opening and grab it when it came along.

* * *

The hot morning quickly got hotter. By 10:00, sweat trickled down Victoria's back, making her jeans stick to her legs. She and Lang had only been out for an hour yet already she was thirsty and aching for a break.

The long, restless night had left her mind in a haze and her body weak. Half of it she'd spent trying to come up with reasons to cancel the ride. The other half, she'd spent trying to memorize every detail of Lang's face—and body.

She slowed Sasabe to a walk as they reached a twisted mountain pass, casting a glance over her shoulder. Lang had his hat pulled down, so she couldn't see if he appeared as worn out as she felt.

As she started to turn back around, he asked, "You ready for a break?"

The tight twists commanded all her attention so she pulled Sasabe to a stop before replying. "That okay with you?"

Lang pushed his hat back, letting the sun shine across his rugged face. "How about we pull off at the top of that next hill? Next to the stream."

She knew the spot. It overlooked The Circle Cat. She nodded, turning back around and nudging Sasabe onward.

As her mount picked its way up the rocky slope, Victoria concentrated on keeping the reins loose enough to allow the mare freedom to find her own way. The morning buzzed with heat and friction. Few birds flew overhead. Even the cactuses looked hot and uncomfortable.

Even though she was anxious to dismount, she didn't look forward to being alone with Lang. They hadn't talked about him leaving yet but Victoria figured his departure was on his mind too.

The still air was so thick that the gentle clomp of the horses' hooves and the occasional roll of a rock did little to break up the quiet. Victoria watched Sasabe's mane bounce as the animal kept its head low for balance.

By the time the last bend came into view, the entire back of Victoria's shirt was stuck to her. The damp material clung to her body, holding in the heat and making her plain miserable.

She guided Sasabe over to the side of the trail, then pulled the horse to a stop beside a scraggly pine. The combination of hillside pines and rocks provided barely enough shade to make a difference in temperature. Victoria swung out of the saddle and hit the ground with a heavy thump. With a few quick movements, she removed the saddle and set it aside.

She led her horse behind the clearing to a copse of trees where a shallow stream ran. Soon, Lang brought his horse to the creek. Victoria and Lang waited while the animals drank their fill. Once Sasabe was done, Victoria led the horse over to a low pine branch, looped the reins over and then stepped over to her saddle pack.

When she reached for the wide leather flap, Lang's hand brushed against hers. She jerked back with a start, instantly wishing she hadn't, because her hip bumped his thigh. The temperature in the air was nothing compared to the hot wave that shot through her.

He set his hand on her waist to steady her, his husky voice whispered across her cheek, making her shiver. "I'll get the water for us."

Being close to him felt perfect. So right. The two of them were in sync, wanting the same thing. Why didn't he turn her around and kiss her? Or come close enough to press his solid body to hers?

Stupid fear, that's why.

She'd had enough of that. "I'm not like Lori Anne, Lang," she said over her shoulder.

His hand stayed on her hip, his body still, tense. "What do you know about Lori Anne?" he asked softly.

She wrapped her fingers over his, tilted back to rest her head against his solid chest. "Vince told me."

Lang's voice took on an edge but still he didn't move away. "He should've kept his fancy mouth shut."

Ignoring his tone, she said, "I asked about you. He wasn't going to tell me anything but I made him." After taking a shallow breath, knowing that this might be her only chance to say what she had on her mind, she continued. "I'm glad he did tell me because now I understand."

"Understand that you're planning on doing the same thing she did? Using me? Taking off after you're done with me, trotting into some other guy's arms?" He pulled his hand out from under hers and backed away.

But when she spun around, she caught a glimmer of conflict in his eyes as he tried to make his next words a joke. "I'm not a bus stop."

He moved to the flat spot where the ground

135

dropped off and she followed. In the valley below, The Circle Cat sat postcard perfect lying nestled among the trees. From the top of the hill, they could see everything, the house, the barn, cabins, even the fire pit.

But the even view of her ranch wasn't going to take her mind off what she wanted to know. "Are you still in love with her?"

"No," he replied quickly, then ran his hand over his face and shook his head, his face expressionless. "I wanted to be but probably never really was. I was just like all the other saps who're fooled by swanky clothes and an inviting smile."

Not willing to be painted with the same brush as the woman who'd treated him so badly, she pointed out, "I've been honest with you from the start."

He paused, considering her words. When he replied, his voice lost the edge and turned husky. "True enough. And I appreciate that."

The mere sound of his voice made her skin tingle. And knowing what his hands and mouth were capable of made her want so much more.

She looked into his dark eyes, saw the same desire she felt pulsing in her own veins. They both wanted more than what they'd had from each other so far. It looked like it was up to her to make sure they got it. "I have an idea," she said, slowly shifting toward him. "Stay here, at the ranch."

"Keep working?" he stepped away and shrugged, "Why?"

She turned, smiling openly, "See where things go with us, have some fun together."

"That again?" His gaze darted from her face to

the scene below then to the blanket he'd laid out. "Fun. That no commitments kind?"

"Yep. Exactly." She spread her hands wide, encouraging him to look at her. "If we're both honest about what we want, why not? What could be the harm?"

His gaze skimmed down her legs, flickered across her waist, lingered over her breasts then came around to her face. The grin that pulled on his mouth didn't quite reach his eyes. "That's a sweet, tempting offer and I do appreciate it." He swung away to drop onto the blanket beside the saddle he'd taken off Prickly Pear, reaching for one of the water bottles. "But I don't think so."

Appreciate it?

I don't think so?

What kind of answer was that?

Victoria held back a scowl.

Lang offered her a smile, smacking the spot beside him. "Come over and sit, you look like you're ready to collapse from this heat."

She was feeling weak but it wasn't from the air temperature.

She took a step forward, then hesitated. The blanket looked small with Lang's long legs stretched across it. No matter where she put herself, she'd be right next to him.

Touching would be unavoidable.

He held up the other bottle. "Come on, I know you want it."

Was he playing games with her, reconsidering, or just trying to tease her to soften his rejection?

To be fair, he'd never led her on. He'd been honest with her from the start.

137

She moved closer and bent over to accept the bottle, drank nearly half of it.

He pulled out a bandana and wiped perspiration from his neck. "It better cool off for your ride tonight."

Back to business.

Victoria recapped the bottle, tossed it down, dropped herself onto the blanket. That ride was not going to happen.

"Have you checked the weather?" he asked.

She didn't want to share her troubles with Lang, especially now that he'd flat out turned down her offer. Everything about the ranch was her responsibility. That included disappointments.

He jabbed her lightly with his elbow. "Victoria?"

"Hmm?" She picked up the water took off the cap and emptied the bottle.

"What's going on?" He nudged her again. "You aren't telling me something."

"How would you know? You don't know me." As soon as the words left her mouth, she regretted them—and her snappy tone. She sighed. "Sorry. It's not your fault."

He braced himself on his hands, his gaze focused on hers. "What's not my fault?"

Defeat weighed on her. "I'm going to have to cancel the trail ride."

"Why?" He sat up. "Everything is all taken care of."

"Well, it *was*." She tossed the empty water bottle to the edge of the blanket. "The guide called this morning to say he's got some problem he's got to take care of. Whatever that means. He won't be here until Saturday night or some time Sunday."

Lang's brow lowered. "That'll be too late. The

group is only staying through dinner on Monday." He shifted over to lean against his saddle, then added more softly, "Doesn't he realize people are depending on him? Doesn't he understand what a mess he's made for you?"

He didn't have to tell her she had a big problem. "I'll figure out something else."

A weak breeze blew across her face and Victoria leaned into it. She lifted her shirt from her back and shook the damp fabric. It didn't help. The heat and frustration stole her strength, leaving her weary and vulnerable. Having Lang beside her was definitely making matters worse. He was another thing that wasn't going to happen.

"What're you going to do?" he asked.

Tension gripped her shoulders and pulled on her neck. Waiting for him to laugh and point out her mistake in not having a back-up plan, she said, "I have no idea."

Instead of mocking her, Lang curved his strong palms over her shoulders, kneaded her muscles with his capable fingers. The warmth from his hands gave life to a different kind of heat. The kind she wanted more and more of each time she got near him, the need to have him inside her, bringing them together.

She could forget him in time.

But, her ranch…

"Relax, Victoria," he murmured. "We'll figure something out."

The smell of worn leather mingled with his distinct masculine scent. Victoria gave in, pulling in a deep breath and letting out a sigh of contentment.

If only she could spend the entire day right there.

With Lang's solid body behind hers. She could easily stop worrying about business... and goals... and even the disappointment facing her coming guests.

His gentle, steady massage offered comfort and reassurance. When he stopped, she let him pull her back until her head rested on his chest. The restless tossing and turning of the night before, the hard work and stress of the past days, the heat of the rising sun forced her eyelids to drift shut.

Lang resisted touching Victoria but as he watched the even rise and fall of her chest, his hand lifted on its own and lingered beside the honeyed skin of her smooth cheek. Even in the shade, the sun brightened her face, making it glow.

No matter how hard he tried, he couldn't get away from the truth.

Victoria Marana was perfect. She was everything he could want in a woman—innocence, passion, determination and an unpredictable personality that promised to make every day an adventure. She was so completely different from Lori Anne, he was an idiot for ever comparing the two.

He dropped his hand, scanning the craggy mountains and the drop-off that framed the view of The Circle Cat. The woman snoozing on his chest didn't understand what it felt like to have everything on the line and really be on the verge of losing it all.

She thought she did but she didn't.

If she lost her ranch, she'd still have a place to live, she'd still have a bright future ahead of her. So, her pride might take a beating, she'd pull herself together and move on.

But why should she go through all that?

He gazed at her striking face. She was everything he'd thought that first day but she was also so much more. Her father had given her a loving childhood. He'd also taught her the value of hard work.

If only Lang was as convinced as she was that she fit into the lifestyle she was trying to mold herself into. If only. But he wasn't.

He'd gotten the last chance he'd been looking for, so he'd stay one more night and go on the trail ride. It would be the trail ride of her life—one last test—then the whole issue would be settled one way or the other.

With that decided, he leaned back and closed his eyes, letting the mid morning heat ease him into a light sleep.

* * *

The screech of an eagle woke Lang with a start. He opened his eyes in time to watch the huge bird soar past, coasting on the high, desert wind. He admired the bird's fierce independence. How well he knew that self-reliance had a hefty price tag.

The sun had shifted so the overhang only offered a slice of shade. He took one last look at Victoria's sleep softened face, then nudged her by lifting his shoulder.

She murmured, raised her hand to set it across his arm and twisted. The soft mounds of her breasts molded against his chest, her solid hip bones pressed into his crotch. His cock welcomed the pressure, swelling and growing thick and solid.

As always, the delicate citrus scent made his mouth water. Without thinking, he lowered his head to smell the silky strands of her hair. "Victoria, wake up, honey."

She rolled her head, causing the golden tresses to cascade across his stomach. The image of her lying naked in his arms exploded in his mind, shoving away the reasonable plan of waking her and leaving their secluded spot. He grabbed her waist, lifting her so her face was a breath away.

She opened her eyes, a lazy smile lingering on her sweet, kissable mouth.

There was no hesitation, no shy awkwardness in her gaze. Only sure-footed, simmering passion.

Her gaze flickered to his mouth, then back to his eyes. "I'm going to kiss you, Lang Thompson."

Chapter Twelve

Her words stirred his blood, blocking out everything except the pounding in his chest and the hot need to taste her.

She leaned forward, brushing her tender, willing mouth across his. Then she surprised him by running her tongue over his bottom lip.

Lang groaned and shifted, positioning her more fully against him.

"Feels nice, doesn't it?" she asked, rocking gently to make sure their bodies touched in the places that mattered.

Nice wasn't the word that came to mind.

Reality circled, reminding him what he had in mind for Victoria and her ranch. "This isn't a good idea."

She wiggled out of his grip to slide one leg over him, straddling him perfectly. "One little kiss never hurt anybody."

The tempting pressure of her ass nestled in his lap had him clenching his jaw. If they were naked, his cock would be inside her but he wouldn't be sitting still. He'd be driving in to her tight pussy, pumping into her so hard her breasts would be bouncing, just inches from his mouth.

She'd already made the offer, all he had to do was accept.

Could he take only part of what she offered?

"I'm hurting already, can't you feel it?" He tightened his grip, pushing her down to feel the weight of her ass on his already hard shaft. "But kiss me anyway, sweetheart."

Her blue eyes glittered with well placed confidence. She lowered her head. He met her halfway. As soon as her lips touched his, he tugged her closer until her breasts pressed against his chest and her thighs wrapped snugly around his waist. With her body molded to his, he deepened the kiss, tasting not only the sweetness but her soul.

She matched his exploration with one of her own. The movement of her tongue, tentative at first, quickly changed to demanding and intent.

Heat from her palms spread through him when she slid her hands under his shirt, skimmed her palms across his work-tired muscles. Every time she touched him that way, it made their physical connection tighter, harder to ignore.

He followed her example, shoving his hands under her shirt, then lifting it. But he couldn't stop there. He had to taste her citrus scented flesh, at least once.

The cups of her bra came down easily, freeing her generous breasts. Lang didn't let a single second pass, he greedily pulled one nipple into his mouth, sucking with gentle, constant pressure.

She gasped, arching her back and forcing more of her firm, round breast into his mouth and wiggling her sweet ass against his pulsing erection. If she kept that up, he'd come in his pants.

"Hold on, sweetheart," he lifted his mouth, "Slow up."

"I know what I want," she murmured, "and it isn't to slow down." To get her point across, she rocked against him, smiling like a vixen.

His gut tensed, letting go with Victoria wasn't a good idea.

It was only a game to her. He'd be dealing with another broken heart. If he got what he wanted—the ranch—she'd be leaving him behind as easily as she tossed out last season's shoes. And if he didn't get the ranch? Same thing, only he'd be the one doing the leaving.

Using his last bit of sanity, he righted her clothes and angled back, putting distance between them. He brushed his fingertips across her face, her passion-darkened eyes looking back at him.

"What's wrong, Lang?" she asked, tugging on his shirt.

Rejection shone in her gaze. Heaven knew, that was the last thing he wanted her to feel from him. "Nothing's wrong, sweetheart."

A tiny crease formed between her eyebrows, then that flirtatious smile showed up. Or was it more sincere than the other times he'd seen it?

"If nothing's wrong," she asked, rocking gently to remind him of the solid erection she'd created, "then why did you stop?"

"We've been gone awhile. Your dad and Susie are probably waiting for us. We should get back."

Her blue eyes cleared and she looked down at her legs wrapped around him. The confidence fell from her face as she swung her leg around. "I'm sor—"

"Don't say that." He cut her off, hating her apology even before it was spoken. He wanted to resent her and the way she wanted toy with him but deep inside he knew she didn't understand what was going on. She had no way of knowing how bad it hurt when things didn't go your way.

Lang's feelings where Victoria was concerned were getting more complicated by the hour and not caring about her was nearly impossible. He lifted her face. "I wanted you to kiss me, I wanted all of it. I still do."

The spark came back into her eyes and she swung off him to sit on the corner of the blanket.

Guilt clamped around his chest and he had to pull hard for the next breath. After all, what he had planned was for her own good. She'd understand. Someday.

He got up and reached for her hand. "I'm going to stay on, go on the trail ride with you tonight."

Her mouth pulled tight and she angled away from his outstretched hand. "You don't have to do that. My problems are my business."

The sudden defensive tone made the weight of his guilt less of a burden. He grabbed her arms, hauling her to her feet. "What if there's a problem? You can't go on that ride with only one guide."

"I know that," she replied, pulling away to straighten her shirt and smooth back her hair.

Her stubborn streak was a mile wide. "Consider it a way of fixing the score between us—for the barn."

After a pause, she fixed him with a firm look and answered, "Fine. We'll be even." She smacked the dust off her jeans then spoke to him over her shoulder as she gathered up her saddle, "But I can assure you, I won't need any more assistance from you after that. Everything will be settled when we get back from that ride."

Everything settled. That's what he was counting on.

* * *

Victoria stared at Susie's flashy, red Mustang until it disappeared at the end of the long, dusty driveway.

Hank set his hand on her shoulder. "It's the day we've been waiting for, Miss Marana."

"Everything's ready," she said, stepping back. "I can't believe it."

"Your dad and Miss Susie turned out to be a great help."

She nodded, scratching Promise who'd come over to sit beside Hank. "They sure did."

"Lang says he's stayin' on for one more night."

Victoria straightened and walked toward the house. "That's right. For the trail ride. I only agreed to his offer because I'd have to cancel without him."

Hank and Promise fell into step beside her. "Miss Marana?"

She paused at the stairs. "Yes, Hank?"

"I know this ain't my business," the old man looked across the yard before bringing his gaze back to her face, "But did you consider askin' Lang to stay on? We never did get someone from that ad and well, we'll be needin' another pair of hands."

"He made it clear that he's anxious to get back on the road."

He pushed his hat around, then ran his hand across his scruffy cheek. "I know he said that when he got here but… well, I thought things had changed."

That kiss… his mouth on her bare breast…

But he'd pushed her away. "He doesn't want to stay, Hank."

147

The old man ran his weathered hand across his jaw. "All right. I'll keep out of it but if you don't mind my sayin' so, I think you ought to come right out and ask him to stay."

Victoria frowned. *I did.*

"Guess you do mind."

She chuckled, to let him know she had no hard feelings where he was concerned. "No harm in speaking your mind, Hank."

"Glad you think so." He tucked his hands into his pockets and took a step backward, "I guess I'll go feed and water those chicks of yours. That ought to keep me out of trouble for a while." He whistled to Promise and the two of them moved off toward the barn.

* * *

Lang hung back, watching Victoria chat easily with the newly arrived group. He was enjoying the sight more than he ought to, considering what he had planned for them all.

The guests, nine city folks from California, were anxious to hit the trail and see the famous Arizona desert up close and personal. He couldn't blame them really, the colors and sights were like nothing else on earth and he intended to make sure they got their fill of adventure.

More than their fill.

He and Hank had saddled up the horses and now they were waiting while Victoria gave the guests basic instructions on managing their mounts. Occasionally, he added a comment of his own, partly to clarify what she said but mostly because he couldn't manage to keep his mouth shut when any conversation turned to horses.

"You don't need to worry, Mr. Byrd," he heard Victoria say as he stepped closer to the group, "All the horses at The Circle Cat know the way home. If you get separated from us, you simply let your mount bring you back."

Miss Honey Kalchik slid over to Victoria, turning an assessing stare his way. "Will Lang be coming with us?"

Lang tipped his hat at them both but his gaze focused on Victoria. The eagerness in her eyes sent an expected—but unwelcome—bolt of desire through him.

"Of course Lang will be coming with us. He'll take the lead and I'll stay in the back." Victoria turned to the whole group, "So if you need anything at all, you can ask either of us."

The redhead who asked the question made no attempt to hide the inviting leer she sent his way. "I'm sure I'll need to stay up front. I don't have much experience. I might get lost in the desert and end up all by my lonesome." She practically licked her bright lips, then added, "And I just hate to be alone."

Victoria looked away from the woman to give the group a reassuring grin. "Don't worry, we'll be taking it easy tonight. Right, Lang?"

He nodded.

Right.

Easy for real cowboys.

"The horses and packs are ready to go, Miss Marana." Hank handed Victoria a cell phone which she slipped into her pack. "I'll sleep on the couch at the house in case you call."

149

"I'm sure everything will be fine Hank, thanks."

The old hand ambled toward the porch, Promise at his side. Everyone called goodbye and he waved in response, reminding them all to be sure to drink plenty of water.

Lang helped Mr. Feazel and his two school-age sons adjust their stirrups then went on to show the Byrds how to hold the reins. Thanks to a twist of luck, Victoria got to Miss Honey Kalchik before the determined lady got to him. Finally, everyone was mounted and comfortable.

Victoria swung into the saddle and separated Sasabe from the rest of the animals. "Ready, Lang?"

He nodded, urging Prickly Pear to the head of the trail. The redhead urged her horse forward with suspiciously efficient movements until she was right behind him.

As if he didn't have enough to deal with already. Lang dipped his chin in a curt nod and quickly turned to face the trail.

* * *

Three and a half hours later, Lang reached around to rub the small of his back. The moist fabric of his shirt stuck to his hand and the quick massage did little to ease the strain stiffening his spine. He twisted to the left, catching Collin Feazel's eager gaze.

Joy split across the boy's face. "I can't wait to get to camp and put up our tents, even sleeping outside can't be better than this real cowboy trail ride. Are we going to cook over an open fire and eat real cowboy food like beans and coffee?" Stretching forward and patting Cassie's stout neck, he continued with, "This is a great pony. Will I get to ride it again tomorrow on the way back?"

Why wasn't the boy complaining to his parents? Any normal child would've been whining about the penetrating heat and constant jarring movement of the horse an hour ago. Instead of complaining, Collin and his older brother John kept asking questions about the hawks and admiring way the dust and dirt of the desert blended into the mountainside.

Lang offered the boys a half-hearted smile, answered another the slew of questions then shifted to the right. A weak light of satisfaction flickered through him. Ever since Miss Honey Kalchik had given up flirting with him about 40 minutes ago, she'd been sporting a consistent frown and offering complaints to anyone who'd listen. Unfortunately, none of the other guests shared her disgruntled attitude.

Mr. Byrd waved to Lang. "Will we have time to make it to the top of this hill? I'd love to get some pictures before the sun sets."

"Up there?" Mrs. Feazel pointed to the steep mountain he and Victoria had ridden up the day before. "The view must be fantastic, we'll be able to see for miles."

Little Collin and John punched their fists in the air and cheered.

With a groan of disgust, Lang whirled Prickly Pear around, squeezed the horse's flank and trotted past the other riders. "What do you think Victoria? Can you handle another 45 minutes?"

She checked her watch, scanning the group. The only person who wasn't admiring the clumps of cactuses or the band of clouds stretching across the horizon was Honey Kalchik and she was staring straight at him. A deep, hungry stare, like she was imaging him wearing only a tie like one of those Chippendale dancers. That hungry expression in her eyes had nothing to do with the camp cookout Victoria had promised.

"Overall, we're doing pretty good. If we follow that trail up to the high point, we can set up camp along that ridge where we… " Her words trailed off in the dusky evening air, the memory they evoked didn't.

As if he needed a reminder of the weight of her breasts in his hands, the urgent way she arched her back when he'd taken her nipple into his mouth. The sweet pressure of his hips pressing into his groin.

"Forty-five more minutes of this?"

Lang pulled his gaze from the mountainside, reminding himself he was surrounded by people.

Somehow Honey Kalchik had maneuvered her horse so that it stood nose to nose with Prickly Pear. "I'll never make it up that hill," she whined.

Mrs. Byrd's gaze darted between Victoria and Honey. "You'll be fine, Miss Kalchik. We'll take it easy for you."

Victoria leaned forward and offered encouragement but Honey scowled, turning a not-at-all-innocent smile his way. "Could you take me back to the ranch Lang? I can't possibly make it up that hill and climbing into a nice, soft bed sounds so much better than crawling into a stiff sleeping bag."

"But Miss Honey, it's gotta be pretty far all the way back to the ranch. Wouldn't you rather just go up the hill? Once we get up there we'll get to sleep outside. Under the stars—like real cowboys."

Collin had a point, it was going to be a long ride back to the ranch but Honey wasn't buying. She managed to pout and frown at the same time, all the while sticking her chest out and wiggling.

"Could you take her back, Lang?" Victoria asked, "So the rest of the guests won't be disappointed. Please."

The happiness on the Feazel boys' faces was fading fast. One word from him and everyone's smiles would evaporate like dew drops on a cactus. His trail ride from hell hadn't worked out the way he planned so far, now he had a second chance to send the guest's enthusiasm down in flames.

He looked around at the group.

Who was he kidding?

If he said no, Mr. Feazel and Mr. Byrd would probably volunteer to carry Honey up the mountain on their backs so they could continue the ride. And she'd probably end up liking it.

He shrugged, nodding with defeat.

Honey shimmed in the saddle as she sighed. "Oh, thank you, Lang. You're just the man I need."

Lang avoided Victoria's gaze as he spun Prickly Pear away from the guests and started back to the ranch with Honey right by his side.

* * *

By the time Lang peeled Miss Honey off him and reached the campsite, most of the guests were bedded down for the night. Only Victoria and the Byrds sat by the campfire, talking softly and staring at the thin wisps of smoke trailing into the black sky.

153

Instead of greeting them, he pulled off Prickly Pear's saddle and led the animal down to the stream for a drink.

Darkness surrounded him when he got to the water. Alone. It was exactly what he'd wanted and it was what waited for him down the road. That suited him fine. That constant ache Victoria gave him was worse than a bad tooth and harder to cure.

When he'd left his hometown, being separated from everyone he knew and everything he'd ever cared about seemed like the only answer to the despair that chased him. Now his future loomed ahead even more dull than his past.

The sounds of the night echoed and mocked his restlessness. After Prickly Pear dropped to drink, he moved to a low spot, bent to splash his face.

The cool stream water did little to ease the heat of the day that lingered in his heart and pounded through his veins. Relief would be a long time coming. He splashed his cheeks again and then rested his wet hands on his thighs, staring down at the glimmering water rushing by.

He had to forget about Victoria, the ranch. The Circle Cat was her place, she belonged there. Not him.

Prickly Pear nudged him, making him realize he'd been squatted by the stream for several minutes. "Okay, let's go find the others. I know you're tired."

Cassie nickered as they approached.

"For such a small thing you sure have a lot to say."

Lang scratched Cassie's neck, got Prickly Pear settled, then approached the campfire. Low embers glowed in the night, nobody was in sight. He dropped onto a smooth patch of dirt, leaned against a boulder. A sigh of relief rolled out of him. The rock was warm from the flames and eased some of the strain of being in the saddle all day.

Victoria had done what she'd set out to do. He'd been wasting his time trying to get the ranch from her.

She'd proven herself time and again and stolen his heart in the process. Leaving tomorrow would be damn hard but he'd be getting out while the getting was good. He had a shred of pride and some sizzling memories to keep him company during the lonesome nights headed his way.

He had to admit, Victoria was different from Lori Anne. Sure, she'd come from a wealthy background but she wasn't spoiled or lazy. She didn't expect things to fall in her lap.

Every time he'd cooked up a new idea to send her packing, she'd come back harder and more determined than ever. That sassy spark in her eyes—he'd miss that. Along with everything else about her.

Even though she'd asked him to stay, she'd also made it clear her plans didn't really include him. Just what he had to offer for the moment. And he wasn't stupid enough to think she'd change anytime soon. He might as well spend eternity kicking dirt clods and spitting tobacco juice.

Lang turned away from the campfire's low flames but couldn't get away from the images of Victoria flashing through his mind. Not just the hot ones, like her hosing down the horses in the damn wet t-shirt, but also the every day images, like her feeding those peeping chicks. Thing was, to him she was sexy no matter what she was doing. And he wanted her more

155

and more every time he looked at her. But on his terms, not hers.

"Lang?"

Victoria's voice barely got through the lust he was trying so hard to pen in.

"Lang?" She stepped closer, her hair sweeping back from the breeze. "I was worried. I set up your tent… "

She knelt beside him, grabbing his forearm. "What is it? Is something wrong with Hank? Did we overwork the horses? Did you get Honey back to the ranch okay?"

He raised one hand to trace the worried curve of her eyebrows. Sometime between the time he touched the fine arches and the second he looked into her eyes, the air between them thickened and pulled him in.

He reached out and grabbed her, slamming her generous body against his hard, weary muscles, then tucked her neatly into his lap. She fitted perfectly. "Everything is fine," he replied, nuzzling her neck. "Hank was on the porch, listening to baseball and feeding Promise cookies, all the horses are settled for the night and Miss Honey Kalchik… Well, she's not *happy* but I did get her back to the ranch okay."

Victoria relaxed but her fist was still holding a wad of his shirt. The sight made him chuckle.

From under her thick lashes, she looked at him with suspicious eyes. "You laugh at the strangest times."

"I was thinking how delicate your fingers look." He answered, then kissed her knuckles.

"That's funny?"

He wrapped one arm around her shoulders. "When you consider I've seen you haul wood like a lumberjack and swing a hammer like a professional."

Half of her mouth curved up. "I always liked to work beside my father. Even when I was a little kid. My sister used to tease me about being covered with bruises and sawdust."

Images of her determined efforts flashed through his mind. "I've never known a woman like you. One who tries as hard as you, who's willing to work for what she wants and I… "

He realized in an instant how true the statement was. And how dangerous the words he hadn't said out loud were.

"Hard work?" She shrugged, not catching on to what he'd been about to say. "It's no big deal."

"Not many people have the determination to keep going when things get hard. Especially people like you, who don't really have to."

"People like me?" She shifted back, pushing his arm off her shoulders.

"I don't mean that in a negative way, Victoria." Why couldn't he shut up for once? He should've been glad for the distance his comment put between them, instead of offering an off-handed apology.

She studied him, honest pleasure bringing light to her face as she realized what he'd actually been getting at. "You've changed your mind about me being a useless, spoiled, rich girl?"

Admitting that was going to put him in tricky territory and that was place he didn't want to go. He needed solid dependable ground. Not some swampland that was going to trick him into taking another step so it could swallow him whole so he tiptoed around the truth. "It doesn't matter what I think."

Chapter Thirteen

Victoria got to her feet.

Lang's attitude was flickering more than the flames in the campfire. Did he respect her? Did he care about her or not? Not knowing would be worse than getting an answer she didn't want.

He interrupted her thoughts, "You didn't care what I thought when I got here."

She was losing patience with his keep-it-bottled-up method of living. Too many questions tripped through her and she wanted answers.

Would every man she pursued make her feel like this? Shivering beneath the desert sun and melting into the sheets during the cool nights, desperate for her next breath but thrilled to be alive?

Or did she and Lang have some special, unique connection?

How was she ever going to find out if he kept pulling back?

Shoving her shoulders back and rallying her confidence, she reminded herself she'd gotten this far with him, she'd get answers whether he wanted to deliver them or not. "Things have changed since then."

Arching back and crossing his arms behind his head, he eyed her slyly. "You aren't out for a good time anymore?"

That again?

What did that have to do with anything? Why couldn't he stick to the conversation?

There had to be a way to provoke him into telling her—or better yet, showing her—how he felt for her.

If he felt for her.

Tipping her head casually and starting her approach slowly, she said, "You didn't think much of the ranch when you first got here, look how everything turned out. I did exactly what I said I was going to do, get the place up and running and filled with guests.

"I don't see why you keep implying that the *only* thing I'm interested in is a 'good time'. If that was the case, you can be sure I would've already had one, done that, I mean." With a glance down her nose, she added, "But maybe, just because you seem to think it's so gosh darn important, I'll move it to the top of my to-do list. Once you're out of here I won't have any trouble finding some other cowboy to take your place. Maybe I'll start by going back to that auction lot and—"

"Victoria, you don't know what you're talking about." He leapt up, planting himself in front of her, his legs bracketing hers. The heat of his body poured over her, even though his hands stayed at his sides. Naked longing flickered in his eyes.

He wanted her, physically.

But was that all?

"Stop talking like that." The rasp of his voice made her turn liquid with want. "Because you're not that kind of girl."

Oh but with him right there, his heat caressing her body, she *felt* like that kind. "How would you know?" she taunted with a rough whisper.

159

"I know, that's all," he growled, his gaze taking in all of her at once, as though he hoped to find proof on her feverish skin.

Leaning in, brushing her breasts against him until her nipples pebbled, she said, "You don't know everything, Lang Thompson."

Possessively, he set his hands on her waist and curved his fingers tightly around her hipbones. "Promise me you'll forget that stuff about adventures and one-night stands. Stay away from that auction lot. Be happy running the ranch, taking care of the guests."

His constant mixed signals were making her crazy. "I'm not promising anything. You—"

The kiss started out strong and hard, then softened as the rough pads of his thumbs caressed the flushed skin of her neck, skimmed across her jaw. Strength drained from Victoria's legs, she sagged against him, craving his power and virility.

Wanting him.

The firm grip of his hands, the tender but determined way his mouth moved across hers and distinct smell of his skin—it was all so right, so perfect. She rose up, curving her arms around his neck, pulling herself to him. Her breasts, soft and yielding, pressed into the solid lines of his chest.

A sigh of sheer pleasure drifted out of her throat.

Lang jerked back, letting her go. "See? I told you, you're not that kind of girl."

Victoria stumbled, staring at him, wide-eyed and aching. "Are you kidding? That was fantastic."

His thirsty gaze poured across her, he muttered, "What would you know?"

Her breath was shallow, her heart pounding in her chest. "Enough to know what I want."

"And what's that?" he asked, his arms hanging ready at his sides, as though if she said just the right thing he'd grab her again, kissing her soundly and making her whole.

And with that realization, she knew exactly what she wanted.

Him.

Falling hard for a man with his emotions under lock and key hadn't been part of her plan, but Victoria was learning to take opportunities where they existed. If Lang would give her one night of passion, if that was all she could get, she'd take it.

The moment was there, all she had to do was reach out and grab it. With both hands.

Victoria swayed toward him, then stalled when she saw something in his gaze.

Uncertainty?

How could that be?

She'd never been more certain about anything in her life. But she wasn't desperate and she didn't have to take whatever she could get. When she gave herself to a man, he would know too, that they were a perfect match, even if only for that moment in time.

"I already told you what I want," she whispered, reaching for his shoulders. "Success. On my own. And excitement. Also," she ran her hands down his arms, let go when his fingers brushed his wrists, "on my terms".

The words tugged between them, impossibly pulling them together yet pushing them apart at the same time.

"Right now, I want you, Lang." She reached for him again but he grabbed her first, hauling her away

161

from the open campsite, over rocks and jumping fallen branches. She trailed willingly beside him, deeper into the night, leaving any hesitation or regrets behind and bringing dizzy expectation along.

He snatched a saddle blanket, then tugged her along until reaching the secluded river bank.

"You sure about this?" he asked between ragged breaths, dropping the blanket at his feet.

Her body throbbed with sexual heat. "Absolutely."

One hundred percent.

The single word was all he needed. In a flash he had her off her wobbly legs, onto the ground.

The hard curve of his collarbone, the warm strength of his stomach, the solid, tight bend of his arms, she mewled in frustration because she couldn't touch him everywhere at once.

He responded with soft, soothing sounds. The deep, male rumble in his chest only made her quivers tighter and more needy.

"Lift your shoulders, Victoria."

Sensations, wild and intense, coursed through her when his hands slipped her t-shirt over her head.

"Oh, sweetheart," he murmured, running a trail of kisses down her neck, sweeping his hands down her back. "Your skin, your smell… "

He went to work on her bra hook, never taking his mouth from her skin, marking her as his.

With a sharp tug, he slipped down her bra straps, tossed the scrap of lace carelessly onto the ground. He paused, gazing at her bare skin, glowing under the moonlight, then pushed one breast up and tasted the tight tip.

White hot bolts of pleasure speared through

162

Victoria, she whimpered with need. With fumbling but determined movements, she loosened the top button of his jeans, then worked her way down until the full, hard, length of his penis pressed into her hands.

Absolutely delicious.

"Sweetheart, you sure you know what you're getting into here?" he managed between quick breaths.

Every inch of her screamed yes.

A wide, feline smile spread across her face as she replied, "Stop talking and kiss me, you stupid cowboy."

He devoured her in one, long demanding kiss, his tongue sweeping possessively into her mouth before turning his attention back to her neck, then dropping between her breasts.

The night air circled around her bare skin, making her shiver in the trail of the searing kisses Lang pressed over her breasts and across her stomach.

Together they struggled with the snap on her jeans, their fingers criss-crossing in the process. He pulled away but so did she, then they reached for the button at the same time, their fingers intertwining.

Finally, they fell back to laughing.

"Let me," she insisted, pushing his hands out of the away so she could tug off her pants while he made a joke about carrying a pair of "get-lucky" condoms in his wallet.

While he tore at his jeans and briefs, she wiggled out of her panties.

Moving over to kneel in front of him, she unbuttoned his shirt then swept her hands across his chest. "I love watching you work Lang. Everything you do looks so sexy, it's all I can think about. But you already know that, right?"

She pushed his shirt off his shoulders then tugged at the sleeves to pull it all the way off.

He moaned, deep in his throat, easing her back and letting his insatiable gaze rake across her naked body. "You're even more perfect than I imagined."

Her heart soared, he had thought about her, but she shoved the emotion aside. This was about the moment, not about tomorrow or the days after that. She had to be satisfied with what they could share in one single night.

Rays of moonlight caressed Lang's naked body, the warm light skimming over his lean, work hard torso as he knelt between her legs, sheathing his solid cock. Victoria's gaze crept lower, stopping to consume his masculine beauty. Her already oversensitive center turned liquid as she admired his large, jutting erection and powerful thighs that promised to deliver strong, deep thrusts.

She reached for him but he held back, guiding her hands across his thighs as he angled himself over her, placing tiny kisses across her stomach.

But she didn't need tender affection or romance, she needed him deep inside her, pounding hard, bringing them together.

Again she reached for him, pulling hard until their bodies nearly fused. The tip of his penis pressed against her clit, promising sweet torture and an explosive release.

Instinctively, she spread her legs wider, begging him for more because at that moment she ached to give everything she had.

The last shred of her sanity fell away when he nuzzled her gently and drove deep into her with one demanding thrust. Her breath broke into gasps as he filled her completely, like nothing she'd ever known.

But he was moving too slowly so she bucked against him, thrusting her hips sharply.

He responded by continuing to pump into her at the same steady pace. "We're doing this my way, cowgirl, so you might as well slow down."

Again and again he drove into her, his cock getting impossibly bigger with each stroke.

Sensations hammered through her, making her frantic and harried. She struggled beneath him, wrapping her legs behind his back to get closer. "Lang, now… I… "

Tendrils of fire burned hot, swirling deep within her and she clung to Lang, desperate for more of his hot, hard sex, yet at the same time desperate for release. "Please, I-I—"

"Shh," he hushed her with soft, wet kiss. "I've got what you need." He rose up on his elbows, speeding his movements as he angled his hips to increase the pressure on her clit.

Finally, sweet, wild tremors shook through her and she threw her head back, arching into him and gasping for breath. His release followed on the heels of hers and he growled as his body shuddered.

When his penis finally stopped pulsing, he dropped onto her, pulling the blanket over them. She wrapped her arms tightly around him, holding him close, letting him know that with her he would always be wanted and loved.

***

Lang awoke to the sight of Victoria kneeling beside him, sliding a condom over his jutting erection. With the misty moonlight flowing over her bare shoulders, curling over the soft, pale skin of her breasts, she could have been a dream. It would've been better—easier to let her go—if she were fantasy, but he knew she wasn't. Just as he knew there was no way in hell he was going pass up the opportunity to make love to her again.

Looking at her with half-closed eyes, he lifted his hips to make her work easier. "Any time you want to wake me up this way, darlin' you just go right ahead."

She paused, her eyebrows tight, then the tension in her forehead vanished. "You don't feel like I'm taking advantage?" she asked, dropping one hand to cup his balls.

His cock bobbed in response and he reached for Victoria but she scooted away.

"So now you're going to be a tease?"

"Oh no, I'm not near done." She crept back toward him on her hands and knees, her gaze wide as she stared at his ramrod shaft. "We did things your way before, this time… " She swung one slender leg over him and positioned her hot pussy just above his stiff cock, grinning down at him with obvious appreciation for the control she had over him.

"Give you an idea?" she asked, skimming her wet clit over his tip.

He thrust up, trying to get inside her but she rocked forward, a sassy glimmer in her eyes as her breasts bounced near his mouth, tempting him.

"My way, cowboy," she whispered, smiling down at him then running her tongue over her soft lips.

Damn. She was changing right before his eyes,

getting more confident, turning into an even sexier, more demanding version of herself.

She wiggled above him, arching, leaning back and showing off her gorgeous, round breasts.

He watched, his cock swelling even harder as he realized he was the one who'd brought the change out in her but he wasn't going to be around to discover what came next. He was going to get what he wanted—solitude—and she would get whatever she wanted—even if what she wanted was another man.

"See something you like?" She reached up, playfully lifting her breasts high.

"You make me so horny I can't think straight." And that was how he'd gotten himself into this delicious mess and that was why he'd be spending the next several months, years probably, gritting his teeth and thinking about Victoria honing her seduction skills on other men.

She lifted an eyebrow, swaying forward, showing herself off for him. "That's not an answer to my question."

His personal anguish was just that—his. And he didn't want her to know about it. He'd have time enough for regrets later, when he was alone. He took her ass in his hands, lightly squeezing her warm flesh. His voice dropped as he replied. "Yes, I like it, Victoria. I like all of it."

"I like it all too, Lang," she said softly as she lowered her hot pussy down, arching back and taking his cock deep inside her.

Even though she was on top, he easily took control, holding tightly to her slim hips. She gasped with surprise when he thrust in, driving deep as he guided her up and down.

But she fought back, moving her hips faster, so he let her set the pace, matching each of her movements with a quick, deep stroke. Each time he thrust up, he was rewarded with the sound of a sharp breath and the view of her tight breasts jiggling just inches away.

Victoria dropped her hands, grabbing his shoulders for support and her breath came in short, tight gasps. As she started to sag forward, Lang wrapped his arms around her, holding her, feeling her body tense with need.

He took over, holding her tightly as he drove into her, stroking her hot, tight pussy with his cock, coaxing her body to give in to him. Gritting his teeth, he waited until her orgasm peaked before letting himself go.

By the time his breathing returned to normal, Victoria had curled up on her side and was rubbing his back while he made a joke about needing to invent biodegradable condoms. He looked around. Now that his brain was starting to function normally, he realized they were actually out in the open. "Maybe we should get back to camp."

Victoria rose up on one elbow, seeming to look around for the first time. "Guess we should sleep in our own tents too. You know, the guests… "

Reluctantly, he rolled to his feet and offered her a hand up. She accepted his hand but didn't meet his gaze. Instead, she looked for her clothes, grabbing them and slipping them on as soon as she was on her feet.

He did the same. Within a few minutes he was moving through the moonlight night, the blanket tossed over his shoulder and Victoria walking silently at his side.

Chapter Fourteen

Victoria reached back to adjust the pack of camping gear so it didn't bump Sasabe's side as the mare twisted through the last of the tight turns on the trail. She smiled at the boys and half-listened to Honey's friends, Mary Thayer and Kathy Nells, chatter about the great campout their friend had missed.

With each step, they got closer to the ranch and closer to the moment when Lang would drive out of her life. His leaving suited her fine—and apparently suited him as well. He'd all but ignored her that morning during the campfire breakfast.

She'd gotten what she expected from her sex with no-strings, one-night affair. Mind-blowing sex with no expectations.

Unfortunately, somewhere along the way her physical attraction to Lang had turned into something else.

Something real.

Love?

His offbeat sense of humor and the quiet, steady way he approached life were only two of the things that made him special. Her woman's intuition told her there was much more to the wandering man who'd busted into her life but she'd never get the chance to discover it.

She tried to convince herself that she had no need for a cowboy with heavy and cumbersome emotional baggage he refused to put down but her newfound sexual freedom didn't have the shine she expected.

"Hiii—hooo… "

Hank stood at the back corner of the bunkhouse waving his hat, sunlight blinking across the top of his head.

"Hop down, Victoria" he said when they reached the end of the trail. "I'll take care of Sasabe. There's a passel of messages on that phone machine and knowing you, you'll want to return those calls right away."

Honey, the woman who'd practically thrown herself at Lang, slipped out from behind the bunkhouse. The low, lacy neckline of her blouse fluttered in the breeze, revealing the swells of her very noticeable breasts.

"Hi, everyone," she called, waving her painted nails, "Did you all have a nice time sleeping on the cold, hard ground?"

"The sky was beautiful," Mrs. Byrd replied, "But I have to admit I was a little sore this morning when we got started."

Her husband pulled up beside her, chortling. "A little sore?"

She smacked him playfully. "You weren't moving so quick yourself."

Mary nudged her horse forward. "You really missed something, Honey. But don't worry, Victoria says the cook-out tonight will be just as good."

Honey angled her head and flashed Lang one of her I'm-ready-willing-and-able smiles. "Will you be there, Lang?"

Victoria avoided Lang's response by swinging out of the saddle and handing Hank Sasabe's reins. "Dinner will be ready at five," she said over her shoulder. "Plan on eating big and dancing late," she added with false enthusiasm.

With a parting wave, she strode toward the house. Knowing that the messages could be for reservations should have chased away her blue mood yet the thriving business she'd longed for and successfully built up, somehow didn't seem to be enough.

She chided herself. It had to be enough. It was what she wanted. Right?

It wasn't that she regretted cashing in her wedding fund. She didn't want to be married, after all. She just didn't want to be lonely.

And after that night with Lang she had a glimpse of what she was missing out on.

Now that the ranch was up and running she could make time to go into town. Maybe she'd call some of her girlfriends, see if they wanted to get together. Go shopping, dancing, whatever. Find some uncomplicated single men who'd be happy to spend a couple hours with a carefree woman.

The cozy plaid curtains flapped out the kitchen window, waving hello. Victoria leapt up the steps and crossed to the answering machine. The red light blinked at her but her finger hovered over the play button.

She was happy.

Satisfied.

Really. She was.

But she needed a hot shower and some clean clothes before she could carry on a rational conversation.

Maybe the hot steam would put some sense into her and she'd get back to the business of running the ranch instead of pining for some cowboy.

* * *

By mid-afternoon, Victoria had the picnic tables covered with bright red and white plastic tablecloths and almost everything under control. Because of the heat, she'd set things up in the barn instead of out in the yard. The dense shade of the old building provided more relief than the trees out front and the hay bales stacked in the back and tools hanging on the walls provided a great backdrop for her Texas style cook-out.

Outside the wide doors, Hank whistled as he set up the half-barrel cooker.

"Looks wonderful, Miss Marana," he called.

Victoria looked up from the plates she'd been counting. "Thanks, Hank. But I liked it better when you called me Victoria, like you did earlier today." When Hank glanced away, she continued, "How're you coming along with the cooker?"

"No problems there. It'll be good and hot in plenty of time." He stepped into the barn, out of the sun. "Did the caterers bring the meat by yet?"

A twinge of worry jabbed Victoria after she checked her watch. "Carl said they'd deliver it by noon. I guess I better go call and see what the hold up is."

Hank stuffed his hands into his pockets, twisting his cheek as he scanned the yard. "You seen Lang around?"

Victoria avoided the old man's stare by putting her attention on the cups stacked on the table. "No, I figured he'd left."

He stepped away from the cooker. "Left?"

"Yep." She concentrated on making the words sound easy, "He's leaving today."

"I know that," Hank's tone was slightly scolding as he continued, "He's still around here somewhere."

"How do you know he didn't already go?" she asked.

"For one, he wouldn't leave without saying goodbye and for another his clothes are still hanging all over the bunk house."

Victoria didn't like the way her heart filled with hope so she hastened it away. "His truck is gone."

"Probably went up to get the rest of stuff from the trail ride."

"Oh, right." Victoria was too embarrassed to admit she'd forgotten they'd left the tents behind so the horses wouldn't have to carry the extra weight on the ride back. When she noticed Hank staring at her, she backed away, stepping toward the house. "I'll go call, see what the hold up is with the meat."

She jogged up the steps and slipped into the front room. As if she'd conjured it up, Lang's voice drifted through the house.

"No, she's not going to sell, Cole." There was a pause, then he continued, "I tried everything I could think of, let the horses loose, snipped the hay twine… No, I'm not kidding… I even did the old cooking oil in the shampoo trick… Stop laughing, you idiot."

Understanding flickered in Victoria's mind but she rejected the possibility that what she heard was real.

173

It couldn't be true.

"No, cousin, I'm not going to hang around here wasting more time. I'm telling you the deal is a no go. She's not selling the place."

Wasting more time.

Victoria's heart slammed into her chest, pounded against her rib cage. Her breath came in short bursts.

He'd been scheming all along.

Trying to trick her.

He hadn't gotten what he wanted so he thought his stay at the ranch was a big waste of time. Victoria's hands curled into fists so tight her nails cut into her palms.

The rumble of Lang's laughter sliced through her like a nail going through a bucket of water. After another burst of chuckles, then silence, the kitchen door smacked shut.

Anger and hurt stiffened her spine. A blinding wave of fury crashed within her. All of it, every minute of their time together had been a lie.

A waste of time.

The kisses, every single thing he'd said, the looks, making love—correction—having sex, under the stars—it had all been part of his game to get the ranch from her.

But… he'd given up and she'd won.

Right?

She'd beaten him at his own game.

So, she should be glad.

But she wasn't.

She was mad. And hurt.

She hadn't want to deal with emotions, she'd just wanted to have a good time, have fun.

The anger was easier, she knew what to do with that.

She stomped into the kitchen and grabbed her address book. She jerked through the pages, found the number for the caterer and stabbed the numbers into her phone.

"Don't you worry Mizz Marana, your stuff is on the way," the girl's high voice cracked across the line after Victoria asked what happened to her delivery. "Carl told me to tell you that our regular delivery guy didn't come in."

"You're sure it's coming?" Victoria snapped, tossing the address book onto the kitchen table. "I have to have that meat soon."

"Absolutely, it's on the way. Carl is driving the truck himself."

It wasn't right to take her resentment out on the girl so she mumbled thanks and hung up with Lang's words still swirling around her head.

A waste of time.

Victoria gritted her teeth.

So what.

He'd be leaving soon. The whole episode would be done and over with.

The clock in the front room chimed. She was not going to waste time hunting him down. There was only enough time to get cleaned up, answer those calls, then finish the rest of the cookout preparations.

Then she'd spend the evening enjoying the company of people who respected her. Instead of stewing over a black-handed man who thought he could chase her off her own ranch.

175

* * *

Lang spent the better part of the day alternating between berating himself for giving in to his need to possess Victoria and trying to figure a way to untangle himself from the rope of emotions he'd gotten twisted in to.

Sure, Victoria said she knew what she was getting into—making love with a man who wasn't committed to her—but he'd known she didn't.

Yet he'd gone ahead and acted on his own wants anyway. He'd dragged her away from the campfire like the heart-sick man he was. She deserved so much more. Like a whole man for starters. Add to that a few first dates, some romance and sweet talk and he might've come close to what he should've done.

Not that he regretted making love with her, because he didn't. And he never would. But how she felt—that had to be a different story.

He slipped his hat off and ran his fingers through his snarled hair. A haircut was definitely in order. He frowned. Where he was headed, it didn't matter how long his hair grew.

All that awaited him was an empty stretch of road leading to a stiff, lonely hotel bed. Running scared, that's what he was doing.

During the few minutes he wasn't thinking about Victoria, he'd found himself questioning his actions, reconsidering his plans heading south. He'd been looking deep into his dark soul too.

Then he'd come around to his senses. It was simply a matter of getting away from the sexy rancher who absorbed all his thoughts the way sand soaks up the sun. What man wouldn't be tempted and tormented by the sweet but sexy combination that was Victoria Marana?

He'd enjoyed her spirited, innocent personality at first but that had grown into much more. She'd changed and the woman he'd come to respect and admire…

Didn't matter how he felt. What there was left of his heart was in no shape for loving. Not the real kind that required emotions and a commitment anyway.

The muscles in his jaw clenched involuntarily at the thought of another man enjoying Victoria. Taking pleasure in her smiles, getting a dose of her hesitant flirting, stealing a kiss… getting the same show he'd had the night before.

If she followed through with her ridiculous idea of having flings for fun, there was no telling who she might let into her bed. A woman like Victoria was worthy of more than a series of nameless cow pokes in tight jeans.

He wadded up his flannel over-shirt and stuffed it back into the duffel he'd pulled it out of when he'd first arrived at The Circle Cat. As he crammed a dirty pair of jeans on top of it, a bolt of recognition kicked him hard. When he left the ranch he would be trying to get over Victoria, not the loss of everything the divorce from Lori Anne had cost him.

Luckily, Cole hadn't asked about the owner of The Circle Cat. His cousin had probably imagined some leather-faced farm girl. Lang snorted. The explanation of the truth was not something he wanted any part of. He was having enough trouble dealing with it on his on.

Maybe he wouldn't stay in Mexico long. After a few days he could head back home, see about finding some work. There had to be something there to keep him occupied and too tired to think about Victoria. He and Cole could work out some other plan.

It was about time he checked in with his mom too. He'd call her at the first payphone he spotted. Knowing her, she was probably anxious to give him a well-deserved ear full.

After he hauled the duffel bag outside and threw it into his truck bed, he stalked back to the bunk house for one last look around. A lot of things had happened but he was still the same man.

He hadn't changed.

He was still the same man wanting the same things.

Right?

Of course he was. A person couldn't change in only a matter of days.

He spotted a heap of bridles he'd taken apart to clean and scooped them up. Not that he really *had* to put them back together. Hank could take care of the chore blindfolded. In his sleep.

But it was a job that needed doing and it wasn't as if anybody cared when he got to Mexico. Lang dropped onto a bench and spread the leather straps across the table.

No point in leaving any loose ends behind.

* * *

After Victoria slipped some freshly cut wild flowers into the vases on the table, she stood back,

178

checking everything. The simple settings and typical Western decorations were exactly the sort of thing she had in mind for the cook-out.

Everything was moving along as planned, even so, she couldn't work up a real smile. Hopefully, the forced one she wore would do the job.

Hank touched her arm. "He doesn't seem to be in any great hurry to get going. Why don't you ask him 'bout stayin' on ?"

Urgh.

Back to that again. Why couldn't Hank get it into his head that Lang did not want to be at The Circle Cat? Well, he did, just not with her.

"I appreciate you trying to help but he's made it plain how he feels."

After what she'd overheard, she should've been fuming. So why was there mostly pain settling in her heart?

Before the old man could add anything, she stepped away. "I better go get changed. Our guests will be expecting to eat soon."

Hank grumbled something she couldn't make out then asked, "Did the steaks arrive?"

"Yep." She paused and turned, "Carl showed up right after I called the store. I put them in the refrigerator in the back hallway."

"Sounds like everything's goin' fine. I'll go take care of the grill."

Seems the old hand wasn't in a smiling mood either. How would he feel if he knew the truth about Lang?

Like crap, same as her.

So she wasn't going to tell him anything about

that conversation she'd overheard. "Thanks, Hank. I don't know what I'd do without you."

He nodded.

She reached down to rub behind Promise's ears then grabbed the broom she'd been using to sweep the cement section of the barn floor and headed back to the house.

Later, Victoria carried several platters down to the barn where the guests had gathered.

Next to the grill, Hank hopped about with his hands in the air while Mrs. Byrd and the Feazel boys laughed. Telling one of his Wild West stories, no doubt.

Mrs. Byrd turned away from Hank, her bracelets jangling as she walked. "Evenin' Victoria, everything looks fantastic."

"You all ready to eat?" She set the trays beside the rolls she'd brought out earlier.

The question was answered with shouts and laughter.

"Okay, Hank, you heard that," she managed a grin in response. "I think we better get the food on before they stampede."

A low chortle shook his shoulders. "Will do, Miss M—, I mean, Victoria."

That got a genuine smile out of her. Victoria spent the next few minutes chatting with her guests, their excitement and enthusiasm swirling around her. She nodded at all the right times even though her heart wasn't in it.

She wasn't listening for the sound of Lang's truck.

Really.

Well, maybe she was.

Because once he was gone, she'd be able to relax. Forget all about him and his stupid cooking oil shampoo.

There was no point wasting time being mad. He'd given up, she'd won. Being hurt by his actions was even more stupid and a bigger waste of time.

After all, despite his best efforts to keep her at an arm's length, she *had* gotten what she wanted out of him—one night of great—no, fantastic—sex.

"Chow time!" Hank's shout was met with cheers and the group scurried to make a line by the grill. After they got their steaks, they moved on to fill their plates with salad, rolls, roasted potatoes and a red, white, and blue Jell-O dish little Collin Feazel had insisted on.

"Victoria?"

Her traitorous body reacted immediately to Lang's voice. He leaned against the side of the barn. His black hat so low she could barely see his face. Overgrown strands of dark hair brushed the collar of his brown check shirt. The width of his chest, the curve of his arms looked different because now she knew what it felt like to be wrapped close, skin to skin.

And he knew the same about her.

"Your guests are having a great time."

She glanced over her shoulder. He was right. The scene behind her could have been an ad for the ultimate Southwestern vacation.

He stood still, waiting for something.

What could he possibly want from her? Hadn't he done enough already?

Frustration broke through the restraint she'd been

gripping tightly and she marched toward him, the truth spilling out. "I overheard your stupid phone call. You've been lying to me the whole time. About everything."

When he didn't respond, she crossed her arms, staring hard into his eyes. "You must be a sad excuse for a cowboy if you can't chase a spoiled, city girl off an old, run-down ranch."

She blinked against the sudden heat in her eyes. It was anger, not the pain of hurt feelings. He was a man passing through on his way to nowhere, not someone who mattered in her life.

He shoved away from the barn. The sun flickered over his shoulder as he came closer, his body moving in all the ways she remembered. He glanced down, then raised his head to meet her gaze. "I know what you're thinking but—"

"Sorry to disappoint you, but as you can tell everything is going great. The Circle Cat is not for sale—it's a success."

As if on cue, a burst of laughter came from the guests. The cheerful sound should've warmed her heart but that was impossible now. Thanks to the icy chill of Lang's betrayal.

The gentle nod of his head was barely noticeable, but in the little time they'd been together she'd come to recognize each of his movements.

One side of his mouth lifted into a bittersweet smile. "I didn't lie about everything." With a simple tip of his hat, he whispered something else so soft she couldn't hear it. She guessed it was goodbye.

He spun on his heels and strode toward his truck.

That's it. He's gone.

Chapter Fifteen

The next morning, after taking care of the chicks, Victoria slid the barn door shut just as a sleek convertible crept down the gravel drive leading to the house. The back of her shirt had come untucked so she stuffed it back into place and strode toward the huge car. It was a vintage something-or-other and a flashy one at that.

"Howdy, ma'am. I'm looking for the owner of this place. A Miz Marana."

Victoria's spine stiffened with suspicion. Could he be the person Lang had been talking to on the phone?

The guy didn't look like the type to scheme a ranch away from a woman but apparently Victoria wasn't such a great judge of character. "I'm Victoria Marana," She said, standing in the center of her driveway.

The man parked his car and climbed out. He stood as straight as a man could but his left leg swung stiffly with each step. He offered his right hand as he said, "I'm reporter Pete Haynes."

Victoria went through the motions of the handshake as she studied his face. He sure didn't resemble Lang. But they could be distant cousins.

He chuckled as he scanned the yard and buildings. "Not expecting any media coverage this early in the morning?" he said, handing her a business card.

"Media coverage?" What was he talking about? "I wasn't expecting *any* media coverage."

A hearty laugh rumbled out of his round stomach and his huge championship belt buckle shook across his stomach. "Fair enough. But I had to see this place for myself. I knew the Perez's. Came out once or twice to interview the mister about his rodeo days." His chuckles tapered off and he pulled a note pad from the waistband of his pants. "Anyhow, we locals love dust to dream stories. Tell me yours."

He waited with his pencil poised above the note pad.

"You really want to hear about The Circle Cat?" she asked.

"Sure, do. That's why I'm here."

Victoria's eyebrows shot up and her heart skipped. Her ranch had attracted the attention of a real reporter? The opportunity to get the word out was fantastic yet she wouldn't be taken seriously with dirty chicken shavings all over her arms and hands. She guided him to the porch. "Please, could you have a seat while I wash up?"

"How about I take a quick walk around?" he said, turning on his heels, scanning the yard, zeroing right in on the side of the barn Lang had repaired.

"That's fine," she hesitated, wondering what would happen if he ran into Miss Honey or worse yet found something she hadn't taken care of yet, like cleaning the old feeder she'd bought for the chicks. "I do have some guests though, so—"

"Don't bother them? I won't." He managed to strut in spite of his limp.

Five minutes later, Victoria stepped out onto the

porch to find the yard empty. Anxiety trickled across her nerve endings. If the reporter found something wrong, anything that might make him write up The Circle Cat as a Dud Ranch instead of a Dude Ranch, she'd be history.

She stepped off the porch and spotted a cluster of guests over by the corral. All four of the Feazels and Mrs. Byrd circled the reporter. She hopped down and hurried over.

"But the best part was the real cowboy trail ride Mr. Thompson took us on. He warned us about the tough trails," Collin climbed off the rail and pointed to his brother, "But we're tougher than any stupid trails."

John's head bobbed up and down. "Yeah, we didn't care about how many rocks the horses had to step over. Or how the sun kept burning down on our backs. Or how our legs turned into noodles cause of sitting in the saddle for so long."

"That's right. We didn't care about any of that."

Mrs. Byrd laughed at the boys and leaned toward the reporter. "They're right. The ride was fantastic. We have mountains in California but seeing everything from the back of a horse, well, it's completely different." She pointed to the ground, "If Mr. Byrd was here, instead of sleeping in from all that dancing last night, he'd tell you the exact same thing."

Victoria leaned against the gate, listening to them rave about Lang's trail ride. She agreed. Every second of the rugged ride had been special. Conquering the demanding trails had brought them together, made them feel like a real band of cowboys.

Mr. Feazel wrapped his arm around his wife's shoulders. "Lang showed the boys a couple tricks with

185

the reins. I bet with a little more time in the saddle they'll be ready for the rodeo circuit.

"Lang's a natural trail leader, a fun host and on top of that he's great with horses, wouldn't you agree, Victoria?"

A thin smile lifted Victoria's mouth. They were right. All of them.

Lang had as much to do with the ranch's success as she did. Extra work he'd done, stuff that went beyond what he'd agreed to do for room and board. The patience he'd shown the guests as they learned the basics of riding, his tender care of the animals, even the chicks. The time he'd spent entertaining Suzie with his exasperating cowboy stories…

None of those things would've helped him get the ranch from her. In fact, without his hard work she might be on her way home, back to that pampered lifestyle she wanted to get away from.

Maybe she'd been too hasty to judge him. Maybe she should've given him a chance to explain.

No, not maybe.

After everything he'd done for her she owed him that much.

Kathy and Mary meandered over from the house.

"Hey, Victoria," Mary raised a steaming mug, "Hope you don't mind we helped ourselves to that coffee."

"No problem." She turned to the reporter. "Would you like a cup?"

"Nope." He shoved away from the rails, moving toward his glimmering car. "I've got everything I need."

Victoria fell into step beside him. "You're going to write an article about my ranch?"

"Sure thing, Miss Marana. You won't mind if I send out a photographer will you?"

"No, I don't suppose so. Will the article be… "

Pete swung around and studied her face. "Good for business?" His laugh was loud but warm. "No doubt about it. Later this afternoon okay for the pictures?"

"That'll be great." Everyone back home would see what a success she was, that she'd done everything she said she was going to do. She should be thrilled but how could she be when he'd let Lang leave like that?

The reporter slid into his car and slammed the door. Victoria stepped closer and pointed to the midnight blue convertible. "What kind of car is that anyway? My stepmother would be turning green with envy, I think."

He clipped on his seatbelt and then patted the door. Sunlight sparked off his diamond pinky ring. "If she fancies luxury coupes she would. This here is a 1964 Ragtop Thunderbird."

That didn't mean a thing to Victoria but she nodded with approval anyway.

"It's been a pleasure seein' what you've done with the place. Lang told me you'd worked miracles but well," he grinned and smoothed back the long strands of glossy hair skimming over his sun-weathered scalp, "I didn't quite believe him, still I let him talk me into comin' out just the same."

Victoria's mouth dropped open.

"Now don't look at me like that. I didn't mean no offense, Miss Marana. I hadn't met you yet." He flipped over the ignition and the purr of the engine cut through Victoria's stunned silence.

187

"I'll give you a call before the article comes out. You tell that cowboy I said howdy." He shifted the car into drive and roared off with flip of his beefy hand.

* * *

Sharp, stabbing pain woke Lang. Falling asleep with his back against the steering wheel hadn't been a good plan but then he didn't remember putting much consideration into his sleeping position.

He grumbled to himself about needing to revise his sleeping habits, then as carefully as possible shifted so his back lay flat against the soft seat where it should've been all along. The pain eased up a touch, enough for him to start thinking again, something he'd been trying hard not to do last night after he'd pulled off the road too tired to drive any farther.

Victoria's justified accusations tumbled around him like bales of hay falling off a flatbed truck—unpredictable and unwelcome but likely to happen.

A sad excuse for a cowboy.

She was probably right in some ways but not in the one way she meant it. Because she wasn't some spoiled, city girl. She was a hard working ranch owner, not somebody to mess with. It would've taken a whole herd of cowboys to uproot her.

A couple of mid-size cars rumbled past, probably the beginning of the morning traffic. If you could call it traffic out here in the desert.

Out of habit, Lang checked off the things in his truck bed. When his gaze flickered across the tied down bags, panic swept across his chest. Something was missing. He blinked, looked again.

His saddle.

He muttered a stream of impolite words as he gaped at the spot where it should've been. How could he have left his saddle behind? What good was a cowboy without a saddle? He might as well have left his hat behind too.

He spun back around so quickly he bumped his head on the roof but relief chased away the pain. The hat was in the rack, where it belonged. Unless it was on his head of course.

Obviously, he had two choices. Go back to The Circle Cat and get his saddle or leave it behind and forget he was a cowboy.

No matter how he felt about Victoria, or how she felt about him, he had to go back. Forgetting he was a cowboy would be like forgetting his name. It simply wasn't going to happen.

He jammed his fingers through his snarly hair, trying to tame it but gave up and slammed his hat over the mess. All he had to do was go to the ranch, get his saddle and leave.

If he was quick about it he probably wouldn't even see anyone.

He could be quick, no problem.

He flipped on the engine, then made a U-turn across the highway.

* * *

Unable to go inside the empty house, Victoria headed to the corral. She hooked her feet on the bottom rail and whistled to Sasabe. The mare's ears perked up and she trotted over, sniffing for a treat.

189

"Sorry sweetie, I don't have anything for you."

The mare blinked her huge, dark eyes.

Victoria reached up to scratch the horse's bright forelock. "More guests will be here next week. But it'll just be you, me and Hank until then."

Sasabe gave Victoria one last sniff, then tossed her long mane, trotting off to graze beside Prickly Pear and Cassie.

Unwelcome silence rang in Victoria's ears. If Lang's only motive had been to get the ranch for himself, why had he helped so much? It would've been much easier to get the place if she'd failed.

He'd believed in her enough to see her as a challenge?

If he didn't care about her, why had he called the reporter?

Then there was their night together, something she knew she'd pulled him into. Sure, he'd wanted her just as much as she'd wanted him but if she were honest with herself she'd accept the truth—he'd tried not to get involved with her. He'd been honest about that from the start, had tried to convince her not to have what she kept insisting were carefree flings.

If she'd stayed away from him, not insisted on touching him, kissing him, pressing herself against him, she never would've known how it felt to have him deep inside her, making her body tense with nearly painful pleasure. She would've missed out on straddling him, sliding herself over his wonderfully stiff penis.

But how could she regret any of that?

She couldn't.

She didn't and she never would.

Unless it'd hurt him or left him with regrets.

"Victoria Marana?"

She shifted to spot a man striding toward her. A sudden rush of relief mixed with longing skimmed across her heart but her body's reaction was way off.

He walked like Lang and even looked like Lang but it wasn't him.

"Oh, hey," he stopped, looking away from her to scan the yard. "Can you tell me where I can find a woman named Victoria Marana?"

Remembering the photographer from the newspaper, Victoria shook off her thoughts of Lang and hopped down from the fence. "I'm Victoria."

Disbelief circled his face. "You?"

Had she looked so bad to the reporter that he'd told the man to expect weathered skin and ratty hair filled with chicken shavings?

"Is Lang Thompson here?"

She stalled. Even though he was out of her life, she heeded the protectiveness the stranger's question aroused.

"Who's asking?"

The man took in her folded arms and suspicious frown and had the nerve to chuckle. Instead of being taken aback by her hostility, he stepped closer. "His cousin, Cole."

The man who was in on the ruse? She studied him, not feeling any of the animosity she would've expected to feel a couple of hours ago. "You do look like him," was all she said.

"Only younger, right?"

She took in his dark hair, sunburned nose and long lashes. He hardly looked like the evil, plotting

191

type. While she stared at him, he pulled off his hat, offering her a boyish grin.

His cheeriness was contagious and she found herself smiling back. "Okay," she nodded, "You look younger."

"So," he turned his gaze away from her to look around the ranch, "Where is he?"

"Lang, he left."

"Okay, I'll wait in my truck." he popped his hat back on, stepping back. "When will he be back?"

Victoria held in her sigh. "He's not coming back."

"You mean he's gone for good, completely gone?

She nodded. "That's right."

Cole's eyebrows shot up. "He left with you here?"

"I own this place."

"I understand that but—well," he looked at his dusty boots. "He's not coming back?"

Victoria's anger had nearly worn off but not her curiosity. She stepped a bit closer to catch his reaction to her next question. "Why are you so surprised he left?"

His matter of fact reply started without hesitation then trailed off. "I ran into Vince and he said… "

"So you talked to Vince, the man at the horse auction and… " she rolled her hand, telling him to continue.

"From what he told me, I figured Lang would still be around."

"What did he tell you?"

Cole shifted his feet, pushed his hat back and then stuffed his hands into the pockets of his jeans. "Just that you and Lang were well, gettin' along, if you know what I mean."

Obviously Vince mistakenly thought Lang's enthusiasm for the horses had something to do with her. "Lang likes horses, doesn't he?"

"Like 'em? Horses are his whole life." His broad grin faded and he finished softly, "Or were… until… "

"Lori Anne?"

"Yeah." Cole watched a chestnut gelding in the corral as it nipped playfully at a roan mare. "It's a shame the way things turned out. Lang loved his horses, I mean really, almost like an obsession. And his ranch… it meant everything to him. Meant more to him than Lori Anne ever did, I'm guessing and… " he broke off, letting his gaze drift across the horses in the corral then back to her as though he'd expected to see something, or someone, other than her standing there in the slanting afternoon sun.

He might be wanting her to be someone else but he might be just the person she needed. Finally, here was her chance to get answers about Lang. "You're going to tell me exactly what happened. With everything. You know that don't you?"

Sunshine glinted off the buckle on his brown hat as his head rolled from side-to-side. "If he'd wanted you to know he would've told you himself. I really should've kept my mouth shut."

Victoria took his arm. "Come on up to the house. I'm going to get you something nice and cold to drink and you're going to tell me everything."

"My mom used to get that look in her eye," he sighed, falling into step beside her. "I suppose if I'm going to let the muddy pig in the house, I might as

193

well have a cold drink in my hand and a sturdy place to rest my heels."

Victoria wasn't at all sure what he meant about the muddy pig but she assumed it meant she was finally going to get some answers.

* * *

After Cole left, Victoria curled up on the porch swing to watch the aspens bend in the wind and reconsider everything she'd thought to be true—about Lang—and herself.

How could she have ever thought a life without commitments would be satisfying?

One of the things she loved about the ranch was its permanence, the steady way the land and the animals were dependable and true. How had she not realized she'd value the same things in herself? In a man?

When a truck turned off the main road, stirring up dust as it rumbled toward the house, she froze.

Lang.

With trembling fingers she smoothed back her hair and wiped away any smudges of mascara her tears might've caused. Her stomach turned stiff with anxiety and she folded her arms across her chest to hide her sudden jitters.

As soon as his truck stopped, he swung down from the cab. Her heart kicked up speed as each of his long strides brought him closer. She scanned his face for some indication of why he'd come back but the unreadable mask told her nothing. His dark eyes, usually expressive and gleaming, stared blankly at her.

She swallowed hard. After the careless way she'd cut through his attempt to explain, she deserved nothing less.

When he stopped inches from her, the heat from his body pressed into her, reminding her of his touch. His kiss. His strong capable body moving against hers. And the tender way he'd held her after they made love.

How could she have been so stupid, sending him away without giving him a chance to explain?

"Sorry to bother you," he said, not really looking at her. "I forgot my saddle."

His saddle.

After the way she had treated him, she couldn't expect him to be coming back for her. She'd already rejected him. "No trouble, Lang. You're welcome here any time."

He pushed back his hat, watching the horses graze. "I'll just get what I came for and be gone."

When he started to spin away she grabbed his arm, lightly grasping his powerful forearm. "Wait, Lang."

He leaned back on one foot, staring down at her hand.

"Please."

His dark gaze came up and scanned her face and her throat went dry. This might be her only chance to make things right. She swallowed, forced herself to go on. "I've got more land than I need. And extra space in the barn. You can use it, for your horse breeding."

When his eyes narrowed, she chattered on. "Really. I won't get in your way and I bet Hank would love the company. You and Cole. You're both welcome."

195

He ran his palm across the scruffy stubble on his cheeks, glancing at her with his dark eyes. "You're not making any sense, Victoria."

Lang wouldn't offer her his heart but that didn't stop her from loving him or wanting him to be happy. She wanted his dreams to come true too. "I'm making perfect sense. I understand what you did, trying to chase me off the ranch. Dreams are strong. They make you do crazy things, whatever you have to do to make them come true." She stepped closer, pleading with her eyes for him to listen. "Especially when you've had them snatched away."

A touch of disapproval bit into his voice, his gaze turned darker still as he looked down at her. "What are you talking about?"

She didn't hesitate to explain. "Cole came looking for you. He didn't want to but I made him tell me everything."

"First Vince, now Cole. You sure have a way of makin' men talk." His mouth flattened and his gaze went blank as he backed away. "He shouldn't have been looking for me and he sure shouldn't have said anything about what happened. That's family business."

But Victoria wasn't about to give up. "I know Lori Anne broke your heart, that you're still hurt by what she did, but you love horses and you're great with them. You understand them. Much more than I do."

She stepped closer. Hoping to take away some of the pain in his heart she pressed her palms against his chest and begged with her gaze. "We'll make a deal—you'll teach me what you know about horses in exchange for the use of the land and buildings."

Victoria's heart beat steadily in her chest, silence

hung between them, still she waited, giving him the time he needed to think.

Finally, he took her hand, gently holding her fingers. "Losing Lori Anne didn't break my heart. And neither did losing my house or most all my stuff. It was losing my animals that tore me up." He reached out with his other hand to brush his fingertips across her cheek, trailing a path down her neck. "I didn't figure that out until I came across you."

The thick muscles of his chest expanded as he pulled in a deep breath. He let it out, then spoke, his voice soft but determined. "What happened in the past is the past. Breeding horses isn't my dream anymore."

Victoria's stomach dropped. Losing faith in your dream had to be the worst thing in the world. "Don't say that, Lang. It's never too late—"

He cut her off with a look, sliding his thumb under her chin, lifting her face until their gazes connected. "Things changed," he said, looking at her mouth. "You made them change."

There had to be a way they could both have what they wanted. "But… "

He ignored her stammering and confusion. "You and The Circle Cat are my dream now."

The words went straight to her heart but her brain wouldn't accept them, they were too dazzling, powerful, and a tiny bit frightening. So she cast them aside, shaking her head.

She shrugged. "I guess we could be business partners."

"I don't want to be business partners," he said, still gazing at her mouth. "Victoria, I do want to stay here but with you."

197

"Here, on the ranch. With me? You mean with me like—"

He laughed. "Yes, like that. And as often as possible."

He continued to stare down at her, gazing deep into her eyes, waiting for her to say something.

For once, she couldn't think of what to say or do.

She had seen that look on his face before but those simple words, spoken so plainly, changed everything between them.

"But you just said—"

"It doesn't matter what I said before. I'm *in love* with you Victoria." He ran his hand down her neck, his passionate gaze branding her soul. "I want to be yours, I want you to mine."

Victoria's limbs softened and she swayed toward him, slowly accepting the truth that had been there all along.

A series of meaningless flings wasn't what she wanted. Not at all.

She only wanted Lang because she'd fallen in love with him.

Maybe it happened while they watched those huge flames roar into the night. Maybe it was out on the trails. Or maybe it was that first day when she saw him standing among the barn debris.

It didn't matter when. All that mattered was that he loved her too.

Still, there was one more thing.

"I'm sorry about being so stupid and not letting you explain."

He grinned, grabbing her around the waist to pull her against him. "You can make it up to me later."

She rose up on tiptoe, ready to kiss him but paused. "Wait—what about Cole?"

"Cole?"

"He still wants to go into business with you. We can invite him to come stay here and you two can use the barn, the corrals, whatever you need."

Lang placed a quick kiss on her mouth. "He stays in the bunkhouse though, right?"

"If you insist."

"We'll have to find him a girl too." Lang nuzzled her neck, then added, "To keep him from pestering me." He lifted his hands to cup her breasts as he murmured into her ear. "I know the perfect place to spend our honeymoon. It's a tiny little place where nobody'll bother us." He eased back enough to look into her eyes. "What do you say Victoria, are you going to marry me?"

Love swelled in her heart, warming her from head to toe. Fulfilling her in a way she'd only imagined. She embraced the sensation, knowing that the fiery affection flowing through her veins was hers forever. Still, she didn't have to make things too easy on him. "Marry you? I don't know, guess you'll have to stick around and see."

About The Author

Isabelle Drake got her start writing confession stories for pulp magazines like True Confessions and True Love. Since publishing those first few stories she has written in multiple genres, earned an MFA in Creative Writing and became an English & Writing Professor.

When away from her keyboard, she watches films, especially classic noir, horror and romance, and reads (of course). An avid traveler, she'll go just about anywhere-- at least once--to meet people and get ideas.

Find Isabelle as Isabelle Drake on Facebook, Youtube and Goodreads & @isabelledrake on Instagram, Twitter and Tumblr & isadrake on Snapchat.

Other Riverdale Avenue Books You Might Enjoy

Servant of the Undead
By Isabelle Drake

Her Stepbrothers are Cowboys
By Trinity Blacio

The Bossman
By Rene Rose

His Mob Mistress
By Rene Rose

Claiming the Don's Daughter
By Rene Rose

Scoring with Santa
by Rene Rose and Theresa Roemer

www.ingramcontent.com/pod-product-compliance
Lightning Source LLC
Chambersburg PA
CBHW051650260626
47170CB00004B/1433